DARK ENCOUNTERS

Written By

June Lundgren

*In the darkness,
the light banishes the
darkness*

CONTENTS

CHAPTER ONE

A VISIT TO THE CAGE

In June 2017, my son and I took a trip to England. We stayed in London at the Hilton hotel in Greenwich Village. On the second day, we took the bus to the Tower of London for a visit. While walking through the tower I was followed by the spirits of a bearded man. I had no idea who he was, and he wasn't introducing himself. He followed me from the moment I entered the tower, just watching me intently. Upon entering the last room in the tower, I saw a display of death masks. Going over to the display I recognized one of the masks, it was the spirit of the man who had been following me, King James. Once I recognized who he was, the spirit disappeared.

After returning from the trip, I received a Facebook message from a friend in Florida who wanted me to give her a call. I responded to her message and let her know that I was in London and was unable to call her.

I received a second message from my friend to let me know she had heard of a woman in the UK who was having problems with demons in her home and needed help. She asked me if I would be able to help this woman. I told her to give me her name, and I would message her and see if she responded.

"Alright, send me her name; I'll look her up and send her a message to see if she'll respond."

"The woman's name is Vanessa Mitchell. She owns a house called The Cage; it used to be a medieval women's witches' prison. She has lived in the house for five years, and it's been documented to be full of demons for years. The activity got so bad she had to move out. She was down to living in one room with her two small children. Do you think you can help her?" she asked.

"If I get a picture of the location, I will know what is there and help her."

I found the woman's name on Facebook and messaged her to tell her I would try to help her if needed. Having sent the message, I went off to spend the day visiting Buckingham Palace and the London Eye. When I returned to the hotel, there was a message waiting for me from the woman Vanessa Mitchell; her message read as follows:

'I don't usually respond to messages of this kind, but I felt compelled to respond to yours. If you can help me, I would be grateful. I have tried everything. Even my friend who is a renowned demonologist couldn't help me. No one has been able to get rid of the demons. I haven't lived in the house for some time because of the activity. I couldn't take the chance of the demons hurting my children. I make some money by letting paranormal groups come in and investigate it, it helps me pay the mortgage.'

I responded to her message asking her to send me a picture of the building so that I could see what was there. A few minutes later, I got the picture of the house. Looking at the picture, I made the connection with the location. I saw several negative entities, human spirits, and a couple of dark portals at the location. I responded to her message and told her I would remove the demon within the hour.

My son wanted to know if I wanted him to order something for dinner. I asked him to call the front desk and ask them for recommendations.

"I called them while you were on the phone, and she had a nasty attitude and told me to look online. I found a local place online that delivers Chinese and put in an order for us.".

I was not happy with the hotel; the employees seemed to have an attitude when you asked them anything. I had stayed at the Hilton hotel before, and the service was great, but this one was terrible. When I get home, I was going to write a review and contact the corporate headquarters.

After finishing our dinner, I told him I was going to the workout room to walk on the treadmill. The hotel had a nice workout room with a television to distract me from the tedious time on the treadmill. I brought my cell phone to view the image of the location while working out.

Pulling up the image on my phone, I saw an old demon outside the house as if guarding it. It stood seven feet tall; its body and wings were made up of shades of black and gray. Its face was almost nonexistent, and what there was of it was grossly contorted except for the eyes. If you looked into its eyes, which were a deep golden color, you could see and feel more horror, evil, pain, and terror than anyone could ever imagine. Its eyes are the things that nightmares are made of. If you were to look into their eyes, you would never be the same again and you will never forget what you have seen.

Concentrating, I used my inner eye to leave the outside of the house and travel inside the building. Walking through the building room by room, I was invisible to the other four demons. I could tell they sensed something but could not determine what was wrong. I could see two demons hiding within the house's walls. Another had taken up residence in the main living area. I made my way up the narrow staircase to the second floor. I found two creepy crawlies looking like large, black slithering creatures. I found the last demon standing sentinel by an upstairs window. Completing the tour, I returned downstairs. I saw several earthbound spirits being kept against their will by the demons.

Opening up my senses. I reviewed the history of the land and the building. I could see past events that changed the land and the people connected to the building. The land it sat on, and the surrounding area was riddled with dark portals and a lot of paranormal activity.

I saw women being housed within the building and in an area under the house, abuse, fear, pain, and untold suffering. These women were accused wrongly, with no due process whatsoever, only on the say-so of others. Their fear, pain, and anguish were beyond anything I had ever seen or felt.

Another old demon was waiting for me in the alley behind the house. It knew I was coming but it just didn't know when. It looked as if it were preparing for battle.

Auriel came forward it a brilliant blaze of light, ready to do what needed to be done. She drew her white light swords, preparing to battle with the old demon. She was now visible to the demons and their surprise and fear was palpable.

"I know you of old Az******** last time you got a one-way trip back to the dark realm. I will not be so forgiving this time; I will kill you." She warned the demon.

"You will not defeat me this time, demon slayer. I will kill you myself, and then all heaven will live in fear of me!" He growled low, his voice full of intent.

Auriel laughed, which incensed the demon, and it lunged at her. She blocked his assault and swung her sword towards him, wounding his arm, quickly following up with a thrust, which he blocked. The fight lasted only a few minutes and ended with Auriel slicing through Az********, scattering his molecules among the stars.

Turning, she returned to the house, hunting down and killing the other four demons. Once the demons were killed it freed the human spirits. Auriel retreated and returned her energy to the light realm. My consciousness came forward and her's retreated to the back of my mind, ever present. Once my consciousness returned to my body, I realized I had been on the treadmill for almost forty minutes. Stopping on the treadmill, I took a deep breath and cleared my body, mind and spirit of the negative energy I had been subjected to while doing the removal. Once I was clear I returned to my hotel room.

Back in the room, I sent a message to Vanessa to let her know that the removal had been done. An hour later, she sent me a message to let me know a famous American psychic was going to do a walk-through in the morning. She told me his name was Chris Fleming, and he didn't deal with negative entities; they were not his thing.

I assured her the negative entities were long gone. Since she rarely went to the house and was never alone, she could not verify it until she went the next morning with the psychic.

The next afternoon, I got a message from her saying that Chris Fleming had been to the house and that there was nothing negative left in it. She was very excited and thankful for me removing the negative entities.

I responded, 'Of course, I do good work. LOL.'

I told my son, "You know, just once, I'd like to take a trip that wasn't a working holiday. It seems like I have to remove a demon everywhere I go."

"Well, you volunteered for the job, Mom!" He said, shrugging his shoulders.

CHAPTER TWO

THE PERFECT STORM

Negative entities are constantly trying to conceal their entry into the physical world. As white light warriors, we must always be vigilant, constantly observing the negative entities to see what they are doing. I was called in on a case in which the negative entities had figured out a new method of getting into the physical realm.

Turning my cell phone on in preparation for leaving for work, I noticed a message from Jan, a friend of mine. Connecting the phone to the car, I headed to work. Once the phone had received a signal, I saw the message on the screen.

"Girl, I've got a friend that needs your help. There are all kinds of activities happening at her house. I can sense the negatives; I've been able to sense them since you opened me up a couple of years ago, but this is so strong it almost makes me sick."

"Send me a picture of the location, and I will see what I can do from a distance." I messaged back.

A few days later, I received a picture of the house, and I could feel an old demon lurking nearby. It was a demon I had encountered before. I could feel the negativity emanating from the photo.

The next evening, I started the removal process just before sunset. I could see several negative entities lurking around the home and land. But I could feel something watching, lurking just beyond my vision. I called the Legion, and they appeared beside me.

"There's something else there, watching, but I can't draw a bead on it."

"We see it too; it's cloaked," Michael said.

"My guess is it's one of the first old demons," Gabe said, frowning.

"I can feel something else hidden from us; we should be cautious," Gabriel recommended.

A silent message passed between the members of the Legion. Looking at each other, they nodded their heads in agreement.

"You will need to go to the house physically; there is more there than meets the eye." I heard telepathically then they disappeared.

"Great, just great! You come in, drop the bomb on me and leave." I said ruefully. "Might I remind you; you will be accompanying me to the house one way or another!" I reminded them telepathically.

"We know." They responded.

"You just had to have the last word, didn't you?" I grumbled in response.

The next day, I received a second Facebook message from Jan.

"It's getting worse; you'll have to go to the house." Jan updated me.

"Alright, I can do Saturday. What time?"

"One o'clock, I'll meet you at the Gresham golf course," Jan responded.

"Make sure everyone is out of the house, especially the children and animals," I advised her to tell the client.

I called my para partner, Wendy, to see if she wanted to accompany me.

"Hey, I have a nasty case, and I thought you might enjoy going along."

"Sure, where's it and what time?" she asked. "I knew something was up. My head hasn't stopped hurting for weeks."

"It's in Gresham; we have to meet Jan at one. Something is blocking me, and I can't see the rest of what's there, which has never happened before, and it's concerning me. It means something is trying to prevent me from seeing what is behind it. As you know, it's either an old or ancient demon, and lord knows whatever else is there." I warned her.

"Gotcha; well, we've been resting too long; it's time to get back in the thick of things again," Wendy said grimly. "I'm getting the car serviced for our trip; I'll pick you up tomorrow around noon."

"Alright, see you tomorrow then," I said, hanging up.

The following day was overcast and cool. Wendy arrived at noon, and we headed toward the location.

"I knew something was coming; I just couldn't get rid of this darn headache for the last week," Wendy said, rubbing her neck.

"Yeah, it knows where your weak spot is, damn things," I muttered.

I knew the negatives were trying to keep me from going to the location. They will try everything possible to make it as uncomfortable for us as possible. Wendy's weakness lay in her neck and head pain, which caused frequent migraines. I'm not as vulnerable to their influence as she is because Auriel protects me.

Arriving at the Gresham golf course, we waited for Jan to arrive. Ten minutes later, Jan's car pulled up. We followed her to a newer subdivision. The closer we got to the house, the more I could see a dark red energy emanating from the ground in my mind's eye. We pulled up in front of the house, parking across the street.

"Crap, just what else is here?" I thought to myself.

Stepping out of the car, the force of what was present hit me like a ton of bricks. I could feel multiple entities underground, in and behind the house. Taking a deep breath, I drew my white light force field around me like a cloak and headed across the street to meet Jan.

"Where do you want to start?" Jan asked me.

"We need to go into the backyard; it starts there," I told her.

Jan led the way to the side gate leading to the backyard. As I stepped onto the property, I could feel the evil emanating from the ground. I could see red tunnels branching, like an underground maze, and negatives hurrying through them. They seemed to be using the tunnels like their own personal subway.

Directly to the right of the main tunnel, I detected a small ley line running in the same direction from east to west. I could see the little black creepy crawlies skittering about the backyard, deck, and beyond. I could sense the presence of an old demon behind me. Turning, I saw it sitting on the steps, laughing.

"What are you laughing at, butthead?" I asked it telepathically. "You won't be laughing for long."

Turning back to the tunnels, Auriel came forward and sent a blast of pure white light energy into them, obliterating everything in them. These tunnels are like the ones the military dug in Vietnam so the soldiers could use them to make preemptive strikes on the enemy. Blasting it with white light would be like filling the tunnels with liquid cement. Once that was completed, I turned my attention back to the old demon on the steps.

"You were saying?" I said snidely.

It screamed and glided through the wall and into the house. Jan opened the back door and led the way into the house. Wendy and Jan were oblivious to what was happening. Entering the house, I could see more entities hurrying up the stairs to the second floor. I figured that was where all the action was.

"I need to go upstairs; that seems to be where the concentration of the energy is coming from," I told them.

I climbed the stairs with Wendy and Jan following behind me. I was drawn to the right at the top landing and found myself in a child's room. I could see a small but powerful portal in the center of the room. A set of bunk beds was against the left wall, and toys littered the floor. Jan headed for the far side room, where a window overlooked the front yard.

"There's a portal right here in the middle; I will close it. Things could get a little dicey here if many of these creepy guys try to rush the portal." I warned them.

They both nodded their understanding, and I focused on closing the portal. Pulling white light from the angelic realm, I focused on surrounding the portal and drawing it closed by pulling the light toward the center of the opening. It took less than a minute before the portal was sealed and destroyed. I felt Michael, Gabriel, and Raphael enter the physical realm.

"He awaits you in the next room," Michael informed me telepathically.

God appeared before me as I entered the primary bedroom; He spoke to me/Auriel.

"Father, what is your will?" Auriel asked telepathically.

"Eradicate them all!" He spoke.

His command was so unlike him that Auriel, who was pleased with the command, questioned it. "Eradicate them?"

"Yes, Lucifer called me too lenient, too forgiving. He and his followers have been getting away with terrorizing mankind for far too long, and it's time I showed them I mean business." He said sternly. I could feel the power and seriousness behind the order.

Now, Auriel was all for killing demons; it was her favorite pastime, but something terrible must have happened for God to hand down the mandate.

"As you wish, Father." Auriel bowed and said to the others, "Alright, boys, let the games begin," Moving out of the room into the hallway where the energy was the strongest the battle began.

The Archangels fought with renewed vigor, eliminating the negatives in earnest. White light swords slashed through demons at an enormous rate for the next few minutes.

Once the elimination was done, Wendy came to me and said: "What just happened? The energy going through here was intense; all the negative energy seemed to vanish in minutes."

"I couldn't see what was happening. My guides covered my eyes; they wouldn't let me see what was happening." Jan said. "When I could see again, it made my stomach turn. If this had been a human crime scene, there would have been blood on the ceiling, walls, and floors. All I could see was negative energy residual splattered everywhere. What happened?" She asked, seemingly overwhelmed.

"God decided to eliminate all of the negatives taking part in this abuse. He wanted to send a message to the dark ones that He was not going to put up with the abuse of white light souls in the physical world. The Legion is always present with Auriel and me during these battles." I told her.

"All I can say is wow, the power involved to do this is massive. I wouldn't want to be on the wrong side of the Legion or Auriel, for that matter." Jan commented.

"Tell your friend she must sage the house and lay down the black salt I brought," I advised her.

Wendy and I left the house and drove home in silence. It took me a good day to recover from the encounter. But there were no more problems in the house to this day.

CHAPTER THREE

BATTLEGROUND DEMON

Monday evening, I was on my way home from a long day at the clinic when my cell phone rang. I could see by the number that it was Dave, a friend. Dave is a medium and the founder of a small paranormal group. Dave calls me when there is something outside his normal scope of expertise. Usually when he calls me, it's because what he has found is dark, like a demonic.

Pushing the Bluetooth button on my radio, I answered the phone.

"Hey Dave, what's up?"

"Well, I've got this client, and we've been to his house several times. There's a lot of activity, and it feels like there is something negative in the house. Could you give him a call and see what you pick up?"

"In other words, you think there's a demonic presence in the house. That's why you called me." I said, smiling to myself.

"Well, that is your specialty. I thought you could connect and see if you feel anything." He said a little uncertainly.

Rolling my eyes, I replied, "Alright, text me his number, and I'll call him later this week when I'm off."

"Thanks; I know he needs the help, and you would be helping me too. I'll send you the info right away." He said, hanging up.

Just after I hung up, I received a second call from Stuart, a friend of mine.

"Hey, what's up?" I asked with a smile.

"What are you doing on Sunday?" He asked.

"Nothing yet; why do you have something for me?"

"Yeah, I got a call from this woman I met at the ghost conference. She wanted our group to do an investigation into her home. But the thing is, she's already had two other groups investigate the house. I don't feel another investigation would do any good. So, I asked her what the purpose of investigating again would be. She wanted someone to talk to the spirits to find out who they were and what they wanted in her house." He said.

"Okay, so what do you want to do?"

"Well, I was wondering if you would be open to going over with me and doing a walk-through to see what you can pick up. Maybe you can communicate with whatever spirits are there and find out why they are there."

"Okay, Sunday will work because I have another appointment in Hillsboro on Saturday," I told him.

"Okay, no problem, I'll set it up and then let you know what time. I hope to do it around 1 o'clock; I'll text you and let you know if that doesn't work for the client."

"Alright, unless I hear otherwise, we'll do it at 1 o'clock Sunday." I agreed and hung up.

Disconnecting the Bluetooth, I shook my head in amazement. It seemed like there was an overabundance of negatives running around lately. It would be my second demonic in less than a week. I suddenly remembered God saying that the light would continue to spread through the world. The darkness, would try to keep the light from spreading, by causing an increase in negative activity. God had warned me that there would be peaks of negative activity along with the quiet in-between over the next several years.

Pulling into my driveway, I turned off my phone and pushed the call out of my mind. The next morning, when I was getting ready for work,

I felt Michael, the archangel, who is my constant companion, pop into the bedroom.

"What's up, Michael? You usually don't pop in to chat for nothing, so something must be up." I said telepathically.

"Have you received the information from Dave yet? This demon is a very old and nasty one."

"Great, just great, just what I need, a real nasty one!"

Turning to look at him, I saw a gleam of anticipation in his eye.

"Now, wait just a minute; you knew this would happen, didn't you? I wouldn't be surprised if you put it into Dave's head to call me." Seeing the grin on his face, I knew that was what happened.

"You're going to owe me one for this, you know. I'm not going to call until my day off on Wednesday. And I am not going to go out to his house until Sunday. You know we have to go to Hillsboro on Saturday to remove a negative. I hope what's waiting for me in Hillsboro isn't an old demon. Cut me some slack here; we had the demon last Sunday and another this Sunday."

"Don't worry; the surge in darkness is almost over, and you can relax for a while," Michael said, looking disappointed.

"Gee, how terrible!" I said sarcastically, but he just grinned and disappeared.

Two days later, I called and spoke to Dave's client, Tom.

I dialed the number Dave had texted me, and the phone rang several times before it was answered. "Hello, is Tom there?"

"This is Tom. Is this June?" he asked.

"Yes, I understand you're having a lot of activity at your house?" As I connected with him, I could feel the presence of the negative.

"Yes, it's been going on for a long time. I need someone to get rid of it. I can't take much more of this." He sounded like a man at the end of his rope.

"Dave told me his paranormal group came to your house to investigate. He said he felt something dark there. Something he's unable to help you with."

"Yes, Dave told me I needed to find someone capable of dealing with dark entities. He told me that you are the best. He said to ask if you would be willing to help me. Do you think you can help me get rid of whatever this thing is?" he wanted to know.

"Yes, I'll help you. I can't come until Sunday because I work, and another person on Saturday needs my help."

"That's fine whenever you can come is fine with me. Do you need me to do anything? Do you need any more information?" He asked.

"I don't need any information except for your address. I never like clients to give me any information. I like to go without preconceived ideas about what I might find when I enter a place."

"Alright, is it okay if I text you my address? What time do you want to come?" He asked.

"Yes, go ahead and text me your address; we'll try for 2 o'clock on Sunday if that's okay with you?"

"Sure, it doesn't matter to me whenever you'd like. All I've got to say is, the sooner, the better."

"Alright, I have another client to see before I come to your house. I'll let you know if something comes up and I need to change the time." I assured him.

"Alright, I'll see you on Sunday then." He said and hung up the phone.

As I hung up, I received a text from Stuart. Letting me know the woman he spoke with would be available at 1 o'clock. I texted him back to let him know she didn't live far from me, so we could meet at my house at around 12:15.

Sunday around noon, Aaron and his wife arrived at my house. We talked for a few minutes about the woman's case. Then, the conversation turned to later in the afternoon.

"So, you said you had another appointment this afternoon. What sort of an appointment is it?" Stuart asked.

"I received a call from Dave about a man who is having an issue with a demon in his home. I'm going there to do a walk-through and do a demonic removal." I told them.

"Wow, is it all right if we go along? If a demon is there, you might need someone to watch your back during the removal." Aaron said seriously.

"I'd love to have you come along, and I think he could use a minister," I said, smiling.

"What makes you think he needs a minister besides the obvious?" he asked.

"Because he just texted me and asked if I was a Christian," I said, showing him the text on my phone. "That reminds me, I'd better text Tom to let him know we probably won't be there until after three."

Sunday morning was rainy and gloomy, I thought, the weather certainly fits what was happening that day. We arrived at the woman's house and spoke with the her family, which is what was there in spirit form.

After helping the woman with the the human souls in her house, we headed for Battleground Washington, where Tom lives. It took us longer than I thought to get to his home because he lived in a rural area on the outskirts of town. The closer we got to the home, the more pronounced the feeling of negativity got.

As we pulled into the driveway, Tom entered the garage to greet us.

"June?" he said, holding out his hand.

Shaking his hand, I introduced Stuart and Christina to him.

"Tom, this is Stuart and his wife Christina. Stuart founded the paranormal group I work with, *NW Paranormal Investigative Team*. He's also an ordained minister; I thought you might feel more comfortable with him here while I do what I need to do to remove the negative."

"It's nice to meet you, and thank you for coming," Tom said, shaking hands with Stuart and Christina. Turning to me, he asked, "Do you want to start on the inside of the house or the outside?"

"I can feel it watching us and trying to figure out what we're up to. It's upstairs, so let's begin inside."

Following Tom in the house, I could feel three earthbound spirits trapped inside the house by the negative. As I entered the dining/ kitchen area, I could feel an older and younger woman in the back of the house. I sensed a presence in the covered porch area at the side of the house. Moving into that area, I saw a young boy peeking at me from around the corner. Smiling at him, I spoke to him telepathically. "Hello, you don't have to be afraid; I'm here to help you. I'm going to get rid of the nasty thing upstairs."

"The other people who came here said they would help but didn't. They just made it mad, and things got worse." He told me.

"Well, they're not like me; I have something they don't have," I told him.

Suddenly, he smiled at me, "Yes, I know, I can feel her." He said and disappeared.

Coming back into the dining area, Tom was telling Stuart about the death of his wife a couple of years earlier. "I called Dave, and his paranormal group came in to investigate several times. After the first time, the activity got worse. The second time they came out, one of the women gave me four crystals to put in the house's four corners. She told me these crystals would protect me, but they didn't. The first night I put the crystals in the corners of the house, I found them lying on the kitchen table the next morning. The second time, the one I had placed in my son's old room was on the floor. I stepped on it as I entered the room, and it broke. There's something negative here, but I do not know where it originated. I'm depressed all the time, and I have strange dreams, and things move. No one wants to stay here, including myself. I've been poked and scratched, and we hear voices growling and knocking. I don't know how much more I can take."

"Crystals can amplify your psychic abilities and warn you of impending danger if you know what to look for. Unfortunately, they cannot protect you against a negative. The person who gave you the crystals thought they would protect you. Even if they could, it wouldn't have solved the problem."

"It looks like you're in the middle of a moving sale," Christina commented, looking around.

"Yeah, I can't stay here anymore. There are too many memories here for me."

"Your wife is still here; she died here in the house, didn't she?" I asked him. "The negative is keeping her here. It had something to do with her death. She may have had cancer, but this thing sapped what little strength she had left. You could say it killed her in a way. She's been unable to cross over because it won't let her. She's trapped and wants you to know she helped you find me."

"I've always felt she was trapped here, but I didn't know what to do about it. I didn't know how she got trapped here, but I want her to cross into the light. I think it's the demon taunting me." He said with an angry look.

I looked at him with a serious face and told him, "The anger you have towards the demon is feeding it, helping it grow stronger. I'll bet you provoked it quite a bit, right?"

He looked me straight in the eye and admitted that he did. "Yes, I suppose I shouldn't have done that. I told that thing to stop bothering my wife and kids. I told it if it wanted to pick on someone, it could pick on me. I thought it would leave them alone if I gave it another target."

"It didn't work. Instead, you let it know where your greatest weakness lies. It will use your love for your family to its greatest advantage. Demons may be obtuse, but they're not dumb. By obtuse, I mean they're a lot like some people; they judge by what they see on the outside, never looking at what's inside. You should…." I stopped in mid-sentence sensing the negative moving around upstairs. It heard me call it obtuse, and it didn't like it.

I looked over at Stuart and Christina. "It's becoming angry and impatient and doesn't want us here," I said, smiling at them.

"Why are you smiling? Isn't it a bad thing that it's angry? Won't that make things worse?" Tom asked in concern.

"Tom, you need to understand that if it shows anger, it has a weakness. We can use that weakness against it."

"How do we do that?" Tom wanted to know.

I just smiled at him and started towards the stairs.

"I'm going to start the recorder." Stuart, let me know.

Nodding my head in response, I paused at the foot of the staircase. I could feel it trying to keep us from going upstairs."

"The air feels really thick here, and it's getting harder to breathe," Christina commented.

"Yeah, I can feel a heaviness in this area that wasn't in the other room." Stuart agreed.

"It will try to stop me from getting up those stairs. I want you to know that it might get a little hairy, but not to worry if it tries anything; I'll take care of it." I said, looking meaningfully at them.

As I glanced towards the top of the stairs, I could see the demon standing there, trying to scare me into backing down.

"Ignorant bitch, insignificant mortal, you cannot help him. You can't stop me from doing whatever I want. I will make your life a living hell." It said, smiling evilly.

As I ascended the stairs towards the demon, I could feel Auriel taking over my physical consciousness. I could sense the change in the demon's demeanor as Auriel came forward. I could feel the demon trying to stop me from climbing the stairs.

Looking at the demon standing at the top of the stairs, I smiled wickedly and sent a telepathic message to the demon.

Opening my mind, I brought my soul consciousness forward. (My soul consciousness belongs to Auriel, the archangel, and remains hidden until needed.) "Judge me by this physical body, do you? I know who you are, F*****. None of you ever look beneath the surface, which will be your downfall. You have no power Demon, know you not who I am?" Auriel asked." Her voice came through dripping in sarcasm.

"No, it cannot be; you are not supposed to be in the physical world." it screeched and started retreating as I advanced toward it. It lashed out, sending a blast of energy shooting at me. Raising my hand, I blocked it.

In desperation, it turned its attention to my friends, trying to distract me. I knew calling in the Legion would give my hand away.

A sudden surge of energy shot from the demon as it reached out and tried to push Christina down the stairs. I blocked its attack and extended my protection around her. Next it reached into Stuart's chest squeezing his heart to try to stop it.

I kept pushing it into a bedroom at the top of the stairs. The demon became increasingly angry and combative. I could feel the others behind me as I entered the room. I felt Auriel's power fill me as she held the demon within the room.

"Gabe, Michael, do it now," Auriel shouted telepathically. The two archangels suddenly appeared behind the demon, grabbed it.

I want to find out why it was entombed in the ground." I told Michael. "Demon tell men why you were entombed." I asked.

"No", it screeched at me.

"Tell her or we kill you now!" Michael snarled at it.

"I went against Lucifer, and this is how he repaid me!" it screeched.

"I'll bet he was pissed, and I think If we take you back he'll kill you. That's precisely what we are going to do!" Gabriel said smiling.

"Noooo!" Too late Michael and Gabriel disappeared along with the demon.

Raphael appeared beside me, "Nice work, Auriel; feels like old times, doesn't it, Gabe?"

Gabe and Michael reappeared in front of me. "It is done." Gabriel said, "And yes, I miss the old days."

Auriel's consciousness subsided into the background of my mind, and I was once again in control. My body felt like it had been in a physical fight and lost.

"Is everything okay?" Stuart asked me.

"Yeah, I'm okay." It seemed like it took at least an hour to remove the demon, but only a few minutes had passed. Taking a deep breath, I cleared the fog from my mind and moved towards the opposite end of the upstairs.

"There's an older man here who says he's your grandfather. He says his name is Giuseppe."

"Yes, my grandfather died in Italy. I never met him, though." Tom said.

"It doesn't matter that you've never met him. He's the older man you've seen in the house occasionally. He's one of your guardians; he's been trying to protect you and your family from the demon. Unfortunately, he wasn't strong enough to do much against the demon. Now that the demon is gone, he can help you through this tough time. You're going to Italy, aren't you?" I asked.

"Yeah, I'm selling the house and everything in it and going to Italy to see where my family came from. I'm not sure what I will do when I get back."

"You'll return to Italy and stay there until you cross," I told him. "Your wife is here; she wants me to tell you she can ascend now. She says she loves you and for you not to worry about her. She'll watch over you and wait for you when you cross."

"Thank you. Will you tell her I love her and I'm glad she will be with God?"

"She can hear you whenever you talk to her, and when her name pops into your head, know that she's here with you," I assured him.

"Thanks. What about the old woman and the boy's spirit here?" he wanted to know.

"They have been released and have ascended. I'm being drawn outside. Is it alright if we go outside now?" I asked Tom.

"Sure, no problem. Let's go out the front door." Making our way back downstairs he open the front door.

Stepping outside, I felt a surge of energy from the backyard area. Following the energy trail, I was drawn towards a small shed at the back side of the property. The closer I got to it, the stronger the energy became.

Turning to look over my shoulder I noticed everyone had followed me to. "You have a portal here, but not just any portal. This one allows negative entities through, and I'll have to do something about that." Moving closer to the shed, I laid my hand on it and could feel the vibration caused by the humming of the portal.

"If you want to feel something neat, come here and lay your hand on the building." I invited them.

Stuart was the first to lay his hand on the building. "Wow, the building's vibrating; it feels like an electrical current running through it. Tom, you've got to feel this; it's weird and cool at the same time." He urged Tom.

"That's the vibrations from the portal you feel. Being more sensitive, I feel the same, only magnified ten times." I said.

Tom laid his hand on the building and said surprisedly, "You're right; it vibrates. I haven't been out here in a long time, so I never noticed it before. So what do we do about it, letting in the negative ones?"

"I have to place a filter over the opening to prevent any more negatives from using it as a doorway into our world." Looking at Stuart, I said, "If you place your hand on the door while I'm applying the filter, you can feel some of what I feel."

"Okay," he said, laying his hand on the door.

Closing my eyes, I placed a hand on the shed door and focused on creating a web-like film over the portal's opening. I could feel the power emanating from the portal. "A little help here, Michael," I said telepathically.

"You're doing just fine; increase your power slightly," Michael advised.

Concentrating, I increased the power flowing from my hands, and as I did, I could feel the door on which my hand rested start to vibrate harder. I could hear the broken glass rattle yet remain firmly in place. Within my mind's eye, I could see the filter form and cover the portal's opening. Once the filter was in place, I opened my eyes and saw Stuart next to me. Smiling at him, I asked, "Well, what do you think?"

"I'm telling you that the glass on the door was vibrating so much that I was afraid I might get cut by the loose glass. So I took my hand away from the door before you finished. How did it go? Did you get the filter put in place?"

"Yeah, it's in place now." Turning to look at Tom, I told him, "You shouldn't have any more problems with negatives coming through the portal. I won't say there won't be good spirits that will come and go because they will. But you shouldn't have any problems with them. If they happen to come into the house, just let them know that the house is off-limits. They may come to you asking for help to cross over. Just tell them to look for the white light and walk towards it. Let them know they'll find their loved ones in the light."

"Is that it? Are you done?" He wanted to know.

"No, there are a couple of other things to take care of." Turning towards the house, I could sense an elemental under the porch. "You can come out now. The demon is gone, and there won't be any other negatives to bother you. But you can't stay here. You need to return to the forest; that's where you belong."

A funny, short, little gnome-like creature crawled from under the porch. "Are you sure I can't stay here? I like it here, and there's plenty of mischief to get up to!" it said, laughing mischievously.

"No, I'm sorry, you can't stay here. You need to return to the forest; that's where you belong, not here among humans." I told him telepathically.

"Alright, I'll go. Will you come and visit me?" He asked with a twinkle in his eye. I just smiled at him but didn't answer.

I watched as he scampered off into the woods. As he faded into trees, I saw a group of Indians watching us. One of them stepped forward and spoke to me. "You are the one who removed the evil one?"

"Yes, it is gone for good now," I reassured him.

Turning to the others, I let them know what was going on. "I just sent the elemental living under your house back where he belongs in the woods. As he was leaving, a group of Indians appeared between those two trees in front of me." I said, nodding at the two trees in front of me. "They want to make sure that the demon is gone, and I have just reassured them that it is gone. They want something more from me, so I must talk to them."

Turning my attention back to the group of Indians, I asked if I could help them. "Is there something I can do to help you?"

"We have been guarding the forest, which is our home. We have been trying to protect those in the home from the evil one, but it was too strong. We were told you would be coming to remove the evil one, so we watched and waited. You will protect this land?"

"Yes, I will give this man the black salt I created to protect his home and family. Thank you for protecting the land, this man, and his family. You were brave to help them. The evil one could have kept you bound to him. I know you wish to return to the woods and your ancestors. You can go if you need me; you know where to find me."

"Yes, we know; thank you for your work for Him." The leader said, and they melted back into the woods. Sensing a small portal at the edge of the woods where they disappeared, I closed it."

Turning back to the others, I smiled at them with relief.

"Well, are you going to tell us what happened?" Christina wanted to know. "We can't hear what you're saying in your head, so you'll need to give us the full rundown."

I told them what happened with the elemental and the Indians. Giving Tom the bag of black salt I brought, I told him that he needed to lay down the salt immediately.

"You need to lay down a thin line of salt around the inside of your property. You want to make sure that you go around the shed as well. As you spread it, you will say, in the name of Jesus Christ and God Almighty, I ask that nothing negative in this world or the next be allowed to pass through this line of protection. The salt will keep anything negative from entering your property. You can also save a little to carry on you and in your car to help extend that protection. I want to remind you that this will not keep out the good spirits, only the negative ones. Some may wander in occasionally, so you must tell them they cannot stay."

"Let's pray now to seal this protection," Stuart said. "Everyone hold hands and will begin. Heavenly Father, thank you for bringing us together to help this man in his hour of need. We ask that your blessing be upon us and our families in all that we do. The name of Jesus Christ our Lord, amen."

"Thank you all so much for your help. I really appreciate it and don't know what I would've done without it." Tom said, hugging each of us.

"If you ever need to talk, don't hesitate to call. Here's my number." Stuart said, handing Tom one of his cards for our paranormal group.

"If you have any questions or need my help again, don't hesitate to contact me. Remember, you may have the occasional good soul needing help to move on. Part of the price I ask of you for removing the demon is for you to help these souls go to the light. All you have to do is tell them to look for the light and to walk into it. There, they will find their loved ones."

"I promised I'll help them if they come to me," Tom promised me.

"I know you said your daughter's having some problems. Talk to her, and if she wants help, give her my number so we can talk, and I'll help her all I can."

"Thank you! I'm going to talk to her, and I'll let you know. I really appreciate your coming." He said, hugging me again. Getting in our cars, Stuart, Christina, and I headed back towards our homes.

About a week later, I received a text from Tom letting me know that he felt more at peace than he had ever felt in a long time. He said that his home was now quiet and peaceful except for an occasional soul asking for help moving on.

He told me that he had a dream about his wife and that she was laughing in the dream. He said it was the first time he'd had any communication from his wife since she had died two years earlier. He thanked me again for all I had done.

ALCATRAZ

I had a late-night meeting with The Legion of Light, as I usually do on a weekly basis. The Assassins (Zyprhin, Dedria, Tomas, and Syphiam) were invited to the meeting on this particular night. We were discussing intrusions into the physical world by the negatives. Two incursions of immediate threat needed to be taken care of in the next six months. One was Alcatraz the other one was in Las Vegas.

All eight of us were sitting at a huge table. A map at the center of the table showed the movements of the greatest concentration of negative entities in the physical world. The map was animated and showed the comings and goings of the larger groups of negative entities from the dark realm into the physical world. Blue blob-like creatures represent dark entities; yellow feathers represent light workers, and red stars represent angels born into the physical world. Dark portals were represented by black circles, and white light portals by gold circles.

Portals would appear and disappear according to the movements of the angelic beings and the demons. The larger the black dot, the more imminent the intrusion into the physical world.

"See these two large ones," Michael said, pointing to the one in Alcatraz and the one in Vegas. "These two are the two most urgent. Auriel, you'll have to find a way to get to these two places in the next six months; otherwise, the living will suffer."

"It looks like there's one more that needs attention," Gabriel said, pointing to a black dot in Washington state. "Looks like it should happen around November or December 2019, by my estimation."

"Yeah, that looks about right. Do you know anything about this one, Auriel?" Zyprhin asked her.

"In March 2019, an old demon threatened to return by the winter solstice of 2019 and go on a killing spree. I warned him that we would be waiting." Auriel told them.

"I think I know who you're talking about, the one that initiated the Sandy Hook killings. As bad ones go, he's pretty nasty because he prays on children. We'll be watching and waiting for him." Rafael assured them.

"Alright, I know; take a trip to Alcatraz and Vegas. Neither one of these places am I thrilled about visiting. The only bright side is I get to kill some demons." Auriel responded.

Later, I called my para partner, Wendy, to find out if she was up for a trip to Alcatraz.

"Hey girl, what do you think about going to Alcatraz?" I called and asked her.

"What, hell yes, let's do it.!" She said, laughing with excitement.

"How about the end of May? That will give us plenty of time to save funds and book a room at my timeshare. Besides, my doctor is on vacation then, so they don't need to find a fill-in for me at work." I told her. "I want to stop by on the way down and visit my uncle in Napa."

"I have a very dear friend I want to visit on the way back up from Napa, so that will work out nice," Wendy said.

Over the next week, I booked the timeshare and got us on a night investigation on Alcatraz.

We left early in the morning for our trip to San Francisco. It was a long trip, so we spent the night three-quarters of the way to San Francisco. We left early again the next morning, heading for Napa. I finally got a hold of my uncle by phone and got his new address. We arrived around 1 o'clock and stayed for a few hours visiting. He was 82 years old and seemed to be in pretty good health. I had a feeling this would be the last time I saw him alive.

We headed back towards San Francisco to visit Wendy's friend. We spent a couple of hours with her friend, finished the rest of the trip, and arrived in San Francisco. Unfortunately, my timeshare had no parking, so I had to pay for parking a few blocks away. And as everyone knows, it's nothing but hills in San Francisco, so lugging our luggage two blocks up hill to the timeshare is not fun.

We spent the next few days seeing the sites, including Fisherman's Wharf. We rode the old-fashioned trolley down to the wharf and spent the day visiting the little shops. We were due to take the ferry to Alcatraz for our night investigation the following night. We were on the last investigation of the night.

I tried to enjoy the site, seeing as much as possible, but from the moment we arrived in San Francisco, I could sense the presence of an old nasty demon emanating from the location of Alcatraz. Auriel was growing restless as the time to board the ferry got closer.

We took the old-fashioned trolley car to Fisherman's Wharf the next night. We waited an hour and a half with a large crowd before boarding the ferry.

The ferry trip to the island took no more than 20 to 30 minutes. We debarked as a group and headed up the walkway to the visitor's center. There we received headphones and an audio player with the history of Alcatraz as told by guards and inmates alike.

A guide gathered us together, and we followed him into the prison shower area.

"I don't like this area," Wendy said softly. "Horrible nasty things happened in this area; I need to get out of this area."

She has empathic abilities, and I could tell she was feeling and processing all of the strong emotions that were present from the atrocities that happened in the shower area.

I learned long ago to shut down my empathic abilities because they were more of a hindrance than a help for me and what I do. The demons would most certainly take advantage of my empathic abilities by tapping into them and that I did not want or need.

"Okay, let's get you out of here," I told her and proceeded to move through the others and out the doorway. Once out of the shower area we found an area for her to sit down and gather herself. We like to hang to the back of the crowd and do our own thing because of our abilities it's easier to distance ourselves. Once she was feeling better, she put on her headphones and started into cellblock A.

I waited a minute or two so she could get ahead of me. That way, our experiences would each be independent of each other. That way, we could compare notes at our trip's end and see our experiences. I had no more moved past a couple of cells when I heard a voice from the right side asking me a question.

"Hey, you, will you help us or not?"

I looked in the direction where the voice had come from, and there, sitting on the bed was an inmate staring at me. He looked like he came straight out of an old prison movie. He looked like Peter Lori, bug eyes and all. He was wearing a light blue top and dark blue or black colored pants which are high watered. He was skinny, short, and full of himself.

"I asked, are you gonna help us or not?" He asked again.

"I won't help you if you don't stop bugging me. So be quiet and let me get on with my tour then I'll see what I can do." I warned him.

"Hey guys, she says she's going to help us." He shouted as if all the other inmates were still in their cells.

I heard several echoed responses throughout the cellblock as I completed the tour of cellblock A.

Wendy and I made our way through all the cellblocks until we hit Block D, which housed solitary confinement.

I noticed the plaque over the entry to the last cellblock. I nudged Wendy and pointed to the plaque. "The D is for demon." I stated and we both laughed.

As we entered cellblock D, I could sense the demon lying in wait. "Can you feel it? It's coming from down at the end of the cellblock in solitary confinement." I told Wendy.

"Yeah, it feels heavy and icky the closer we get in." She responded.

"I've been trying to get some video, but the negative keeps shutting my camera down; I'll keep trying."

As we moved closer to solitary confinement, I could hear the demon growling and screaming. One of the female park rangers asked, "So who wants to be locked in solitary confinement, cell number 13? The guys from Ghost Adventures came and claimed there was something negative with red eyes in that cell. But then they're not the first people to have an experience in that particular cell." Several people gathered around the area, but no one came forward to accept the challenge.

Wendy and I looked at each other and told the park ranger, "Hell yes, we'll do it!" We stepped forward laughing.

This was what I had planned on doing anyway. Once we get inside, I would do the removal without the interference of anyone or anything.

Once we were locked inside room number 13, it was so black you couldn't see your hand in front of your face. The atmosphere inside the cell was heavy and negative feeling. A growl seemed to be coming from the far corner of the room. We both turned simultaneously and saw glowing red eyes staring at us from the far-left corner of the room.

"It's in the corner. Did you see the red eyes? I only saw them for a second?" She whispered to me.

"Oh, I see it all right, along with the rest. It's screaming at me, and it's giving me a headache." I told her. "Just give me a couple of seconds. I'm going to be taking care of business here."

"Okay, no problem, I'll just watch the door," Wendy laughed.

She knew I did 99% of my removals telepathically; that way, no one misinterprets what I am saying because they can't hear the conversation I'm having with the demonic in my head.

"Filthy mortal creature you think you can challenge me? You are nothing; you are insignificant; I will make you wish you were never born and kill you!" The demon screamed at me.

"Really, really, is that all you've got? You won't scare anybody with that line, but then I'm not just anybody; I'm your worst nightmare!" I responded.

"I have met hundreds like you before seeking to remove or destroy me, and none have succeeded. I have made every one of them wish they had never come to this place!" The demon shouted at me I could feel it less than an arm's length away.

"You have met no one like me, for there is no other." At that moment, Auriel came forward.

"How can hell have so many unenlightened de-mons and still exist? Now you are saying there were hundreds like me?"

Reaching out, Auriel grabbed the demon by the throat, looking for any signs of familiarity. All the while, the demon was struggling to get away. "I don't know you, but I know your name, Til******. I'm sure you know me, our meeting will not end well for you! Now tell me about the old one entombed under this rock. I can feel him listening I can also feel him influencing those who were imprisoned here."

"You would be unwise to approach him; we know he is there, but we do not acknowledge or communicate with him. It would bring Lucifers wrath upon us. To do this would be unwise even for an archangel such as you." It warned Auriel.

"Thank you for your unneeded advice, but you won't be around to find out what happens now, will you?" Pulling out her's white light sword she sliced through the demon in one swift stroke of the blade.

"Av****** I know you are here," I told the old demon entombed in the rock. "I am not here to release you but to warn you. These other demons have come because you called them to you. I will leave you alone to your solitude, but if you call anymore here, I will know and be back and send you back to Lucifer. And he will make you wish that you had stayed here. You know I can and will do it. Do we understand each other?" I asked the demon.

He growled a response, "I understand, Auriel, but mark my words, Lucifer will not be happy with your interference."

"He is never happy when one of us interferes, and I have been interfering a lot lately. I released another he had entombed a couple of years ago and sent it back to him. It no longer exists, but I have also found some renegades he has been looking for. Lucifer owes me a favor for that." I told it and severed communication with it.

"It's done; an old one is entombed in the rock comprising this island. Lucifer put it there, and I'm not about to free it. I did warn it not to summon any more demons to the island or I would know, and we would send it back to Lucifer in a box and let him deal with it." I told Wendy.

"I was wondering what was taking so long; I was afraid they might open the door before you were done. I'm glad that part is over now; we can enjoy the rest of the place and visit the souvenir shop." Wendy said, smiling.

"Good idea, let's find the shop!"

As we made our way towards the souvenir shop, I could hear several voices saying thank you coming from the other cellblocks. Making our way down to the souvenir shop we spent the next half hour investigating every nook and cranny in the souvenir shop. We bought a whole bag full of souvenirs for friends and family.

We spent another two days in San Francisco and then headed back home. All in all, it was a successful mission and removal.

DEMON FARM

I received an email for help from a woman named Jean; she and her husband had bought a farm in Grass Plains, Oregon. I called and spoke with her.

"Hello Jean, what can I do for you?" I asked her.

"My husband and I bought our farm about six months ago, and strange things have happened since we moved in. We have ten children, and my eight-year-old is autistic. Since we've moved in here, his whole demeanor has changed. He used to be so happy and smiling all the time; now, he throws tantrums, doesn't want to be left alone, and screams when he is. He talks about the scary bug creatures trying to bite him and telling him they're going to kill his mom and dad. The minute he leaves the farm, he returns to his old smiling self."

"Can you send me some pictures of the house, buildings, and land so I can get a clearer picture of what's there?"

"Sure, I'll do it tonight. How soon can you come? There are so many negative things happening here. Three weeks ago, we stayed in the fifth wheel while my husband worked on the bathrooms. We were awakened at almost 3 am by horrible pounding on all sides of the trailer. My husband went outside to see what was happening, but he couldn't see anything, but the pounding continued. The children we so scared and trauma- tized that we hooked up the truck to the trailer and left. We've been staying with my mom while the house repairs are ongoing. I refuse to stay there until something is done to eliminate these things!"

"I have Wednesday off; I'll head out early in the morning for your place. I should be there around 8:30," I told her.

"Oh, thank you so much; you don't know how much this means to us. About a mile before you get to our house, there's a gas station with a little store attached; my husband Doug and I will meet you there."

"Alright, make sure you get me those pictures, I will see you Wednesday." I reminded her and hung up the phone.

"There are several negatives at the farm. Most of them are attached to the land. They have been there for hundreds of years. I can tell you this: they are determined to remain where they are, and they are targeting the autistic boy." Gabriel, the archangel, informed me.

"Great, just great. I really hate it when they target children and animals." I responded angrily.

The day of the removal dawned cloudy and rainy a perfect fit for the upcoming removal. I was on my own for this removal, as my Para partner had finally found a job, and Stuart, my minister friend, was unavailable. It was much like old times when I did everything by myself.

The trip took over an hour, and I arrived before Jean and her husband. I could feel negative entities along the road sporadically the last few miles of the trip. I sensed their connection to the entities at my destination. Talk about a ghost-to-ghost network; these entities were actively connected.

Arriving at the gas station I waited for a few minutes when a 4x4 pickup truck rolled into the station. A middle-aged woman climbed out of the truck and headed towards me.

"June?" she asked.

"Yes, you must be Jean?" I asked.

"Yes, that's my husband Doug." She said as he waved. "Just follow us, you wouldn't find the farm if you didn't know where to look."

I followed them to their property. The moment my tires hit the property, I was bombarded with images of the negatives watching me and trying to figure out who and what I was. Completely ignoring them, I exited the car and approached the clients.

"What do you want us to do?" Doug asked, sounding nervous.

I smiled reassuringly at him and said, "You don't have to do anything; just wait here. Is the house unlocked?"

"No, it's locked up; I come here on the weekends and work on the house by myself, or a friend comes with me. Do you want me to unlock it?" He asked.

"Yes, why don't you go ahead and unlock the door? It's last on my list to clean out." I told him.

Once he was gone, I spoke with Jean. "He's been attacked at the house, hasn't he?" I asked her.

She looked surprised, "Yes, on several occasions, he's been scratched, pushed off the ladder, and locked out when he had unlocked it a moment before and no one else was with him. I refuse to let any of the children set foot on this property until it's cleared!" She said with deadly intent in her voice.

"Not to worry. When I'm done here, there won't be a bit of negativity left, and you can live here in peace." I told her firmly.

There were ten acres to the farm, but the outbuildings and the home seemed to be the focal point of the activity.

Doug returned from opening up the house.

"I would like the both of you to remain here near your truck. I'm going to lay down a circle of black salt around you and the vehicle. I want you to stay in the circle until I clear everything out; it will be safer for both of you. No matter what you see or hear, stay inside the circle." I gave them strict instructions.

There were four buildings, including the house. I was being pulled to the building farthest away from the house. It was an old barn-like structure used for harvesting nuts. As I entered the open doorway, I saw a couple of little minion creatures skittering along the roof joists.

Okay, I thought, *where's your master?* Scanning the rest of the interior, I found the lesser demon entering the building through the far wall and screeching at me.

"Mortal bitch, I will kill you, and then if you're lucky I will let you serve me." Its abrasive guttural voice was filled with menace.

"Really? Think again; I've been dealing with your kind for many millennia, and I have yet to find one of you with brains enough to outthink me."

The demon suddenly lunged intent on harming me. Bringing Auriel forward, I raised my hand and sent a powerful burst of energy toward it. The energy hit the demon and sent it back through the far wall. It returned with a vengeance, dark sword in hand it went on the attack. Auriel drew her white light swords in one swift, fluid movement, and the fight was on. We fought for a few minutes, and then Auriel's sword sliced through the demon, silencing it forever.

The little minions ran through the wall toward the next building. I scanned the building where I was standing and the land below it. I couldn't find anything negative left, so I moved on to the next building.

As I examined the second building, I realized it was connected to the one just down from it by a single passageway. Entering the building, I found several more minions and one pissed-off old demon lying in wait for me.

"Auriel, why are you here? You do not belong here; leave us!" It shouted.

"U***** I see you're up to your old tricks again. I told you last time if you came back, I would not be as forgiving as last time!" Auriel told him in a deadly, ominous voice.

"You dare challenge me? We are many of us and have been here for hundreds of years; this is our dominion. Leave now, or I will kill the physical body you inhabit!" It threatened.

A voice came from behind the old demon, "I don't think so; I protect her physical body."

The demon quickly turned away from Auriel to face archangel Michael, who had just appeared.

"Michael, you cannot tell me what to do; you are outnumbered we will prevail." The demon growled, sounding a little less confident.

"U*****, since when has that ever helped you? Remember the war and the loss you suffered. Do you really think a few of you can beat the two who disarmed Lucifer and his son M*******?" Michael reminded him. "Leave now and take the others with you before I change my mind."

"I will not be told what to do!" the old demon shouted, running towards Michael.

Michael evaded the negatives sword; and drew his sword slicing through the old demon.

The minions decided to attack Auriel, while Michael was otherwise engaged. Pulling her sword out of its sheath she managed to slice through two of the minions and sent the third one spiraling back into the dark realm.

"I thought you had another assignment," Auriel said to Michael.

"I finished early and thought I would drop by and give you a hand." He said, smiling at her.

"I had everything under control, but it was nice of you to stop by and visit." She told him.

"I have to get back, have fun, there are a couple more up at the house. I don't like this area; there are too many variables, and the ley lines are strong here." He said, frowning, and disappeared.

Shrugging, I wandered into the third building to ensure nothing lingered there. Entering the third building, I received an image of nuts being harvested and bagged but nothing else. Exiting the building, the owners met me.

"What did you do you find?" Jean asked.

"In the first building were some creepy little guys and a lesser demon. I removed these, moved on to the second building, and realized that the two buildings were connected, making it easier to 'see' what was there. The second building had an old demon who had taken up residence. Michael popped in briefly to help with the old demon. We both have encountered that particular demon before."

"Is that it? Is everything gone now?" Doug asked.

"Unfortunately, there are a couple up at the house. I will need to remove them, and I clear the land afterward. You have tunnels running under the land created by the negatives to come and go as they please. These will need to be dealt with as well. Would you like to come with me to the house or stay here?" I asked them.

"If you don't mind, we want to come with you. Will we be safe?" Jean asked.

"Yes, I'll have a couple of the warrior angels protect you while we are there," I assured them. Calling out to two of the warrior angels, I assigned them to watch over the couple.

Doug led the way up to the house.

"Let me go in first; I can head anything off that way," I advised Doug.

Entering the house, I could feel the heaviness in the air and sense the presence of at least four negatives and one earthbound entity.

I brought Auriel forward, and she told them, "*Foolish creatures will you never learn, the earth is under our protection, not yours to do as you please!*"

"*This is our domain, Auriel, you have no right to keep us from doing as we please. We have been here for thousands of years; you cannot force us to leave. We will not put up with your interference. Lucifer lets us do as we please, and we answer only to him.*" The bigger of the two demons informed Auriel.

Beneath all of the posturing, a real fear was taking hold of them. Auriel decided to display her full countenance. Suddenly, the room took on an etheric feel as Auriel displayed her angelic body, wings, and all. I felt discomfort between my shoulder blades as her wings came out.

I noticed the homeowners looking at me oddly but had no time to give them an explanation.

"*As I see it, you have two options: either I return you to your realm, or I destroy you. You might prefer the first of the two options, but if you give me any problems, I will choose the second option for you. Take your pick; I don't have all day*". She informed them, impatience heavy in her voice.

"You are but one archangel; you cannot possibly win against us!" The bigger of the demons said, producing a dark sword.

The smaller of the two demons said to the larger one, *"Remember the war; she disarmed several of the old ones at the same time. She is no ordinary archangel, but a slayer. Can't we just go back to the dark realm?"* it implored the other demon.

"You sniveling little coward, you go back, I'm not leaving here, I like it!" He shouted back and lunged at Auriel, barely missing her.

Drawing her white light swords, she caught the demon by the arm, wounding its sword arm. Shifting the sword to its other hand, it attempted to slice through Auriel. Stepping just out of reach, Auriel managed to slice through the demon's heart, sending its molecules into the dark void of space.

Turning to the other demon, she asked, *"Well?"*

"Just send me back if you don't mind." It said nervously.

Putting away her sword, she formed an infinity orb and threw it at the demon enclosing it in the orb and sending it down into the dark realm. Auriel withdrew back into my body, and I was once again in control.

I sensed the presence of a human female spirit in the basement. "I need to go to the basement; there's a female spirit hiding there," I told Doug.

"Follow me; the stairs are off of the kitchen." He said, leading me to the back of the house. He opened a small door on the right side of the entry to the kitchen. He turned on a light switch on the inside of the door. "Do you want me to go first?" he asked.

"No, it's alright; she means no harm; you can both follow me," I instructed them.

Descending the old narrow stairs, I stood momentarily to adjust my eyes to the room's dimness. An older woman came forward and introduced herself.

"My name is Kathleen, ma'am; it's my job to protect the children." She told me, pointing behind her where I could see three small children, ranging from 3-6 years of age. *"I want to thank you for taking away the nasty ones, they would always torment the children."*

"What did the children die of?" I asked her.

"Was a sickness that took their lives. I was here before them, and when they died, I tried to protect them from the nasty ones just as I did her little ones." She said, pointing at Jean.

"There are three small children here ranging in ages from 3-6 years old. She is protecting them from the nasty ones. She said she tried to protect your children, too. Her name is Kathleen. She died before the children did, and she stayed to protect them." I told Doug and Jean.

I could see Jean trying to hold back tears of gratitude. "Tell her thank you very much; I appreciate whatever she could do to help," Jean said.

"She can hear you; she says you are welcome. I'm going to send them all home to God. There's no reason for them to stay here anymore. The demons kept them from going home, but now they're free to go." I told Jean.

"Alright, everyone, hold hands. I will make a white light tunnel; all you have to do is run into it, and you will see your family. Are you ready?" I asked. They all nodded their heads. Yes, and I created the tunnel. *"Everyone run quickly into the light,"* I instructed them. I could see them running towards the light and arms reaching for them. Once they were inside, I closed the tunnel.

"They're gone now; they are happy and safe. There's nothing more here that's negative. I have something for you in my car to seal the land with." I told them, heading towards the door. Once outside, I grabbed my backpack and dug out the black salt I had brought along with the instructions for laying it down.

"You need first to sage the buildings, then lay down the black salt around each building, repeating the prayer on the instructions. You need to do it right away, today if possible." I instructed them.

"Is there a reason that it has to be done today? Not that I don't intend to do it today, but just curious." Jean asked.

"The road that we turned off of has a ley line running up it, which means there will be a lot of paranormal activity surrounding it. A ley line is a line of naturally occurring power; this power can be used for good and evil." I informed them seriously.

"Okay, I get it. So this black salt will protect us from negatives, right?" Doug asked.

"It will protect you from anything demonic. It doesn't stop good spirits or earthbound spirits who are buttheads. The buttheads, you'll have to tell them to get out in the name of Jesus Christ, and it should work. If it doesn't, just let me know, and I'll take care of them." I told them, smiling.

They both laughed and thanked me profusely for my help. I told them to keep in touch and let me know how they get on.

Heading home, I could see other negative entities on properties along a ten-mile radius of the farm. Negatives have a kind of ghost-to-ghost party line, and when someone disconnects a few of them, they get confused about why they are not on the party line. I find it funny as they will find out soon enough.

CHAPTER FIVE

DEMONIC ATTACK

The idea was brought up for a weekend paranormal investigation in Astoria, Oregon. It would be open to anyone from any group who wanted to participate in the investigations which had been set up. The investigations would be held in the Liberty Theater, Norblad and Commodore hotels.

The first night we were in Astoria, I learned from a hotel worker that a local establishment called the Portway Tavern was haunted. I informed the others I had come with about it, and we all decided to have dinner there.

I phoned Stuart and informed him what I had found out.

"Hey, I talked to one of the locals working here in the hotel and they told me about the Portway Tavern. It was built in the early 1920s by a group of longshoremen as a meeting place for all the sailors who came into the port. The guy told me it was haunted. So, let's go have dinner there. What do you think? Do you wanna meet up there?"

"Sure, it sounds interesting." He agreed.

An hour later we all met at the Portway Tavern and went inside. We sat down and placed our dinner orders.

After the waitress took our order, Stuart asked her, "I've heard this Tavern is haunted. Can you tell me a little bit about that?"

"Of course, there's supposed to be a man seen here, and everyone thinks he might be the original owner who died or a sea captain. Also, some people have seen a middle-aged woman here as well." She told him.

A man walked up behind her as she spoke, listening to her. After she finished speaking, he laughed.

"She's wrong, you know," he said, looking at me.

I looked at the others to see if anyone else had seen him, but no one appeared aware of his presence.

"I'm not who they think I am." He informed me.

"They think you were the bar owner or sea captain."

"Neah, my name is William Winston. I was a sailor, and this was my port of call. I had a sweetheart who lived here; her name was Sarah McKinney. She died after I did.

"When did you die, William?"

"I died in 1942 at the ripe old age of 72." He said, laughing. "They tell me it was my heart."

"You do know you're dead. You're a ghost; don't you want to go home?" I asked him.

"I know I'm dead, but a ghost. Let's just say I'm a displaced individual." He responded, laughing heartily.

I laughed with him, "I like that; it's the first time I've received that answer from a spirit."

The others heard me laughing and looked around to see what I was laughing about.

"What's so funny, June?" Stuart asked curiously.

"Well, William here," I said, pointing to my right, "he says he's not a ship captain, nor was he the owner of this place. He says he was a sailor who called Astoria his home. He doesn't want to cross over; he likes it here and wants to stay. His girlfriend is here as well; her name is Sarah McKinney." I told them.

"Does he know he's a ghost?" Stuart's wife Christina asked me.

"Oh, he knows he's dead, but he doesn't think of himself as a ghost. He says he's just a 'displaced individual', which made me laugh."

"Ask him what he misses most about being alive," Stuart asked.

"Tell them an ice-cold beer." He said, grinning at me.

"He says an ice-cold beer."

"How about if I have one for him?" Stuart asked.

William sighed and said, *"It's not the same; thanks for offering, though."*

"He said to tell you thank you, but it wouldn't be the same," I told Stuart.

William disappeared momentarily and returned with a woman in a knee-length dress from what looked like her late thirties or early forties. *"Sarah, I want you to meet June; she's a very nice woman. I think you'll like her."*

"Pleased to meet you, ma'am," she said shyly.

"It's nice to meet you too, Sarah. How did you die, Sarah?" I acknowledged.

A sudden look of sadness crossed her face, *"Our child died at birth, and I never really recovered; then William died, and I was never the same; I died of a broken heart."* She told me, turning to look at William.

"She never got over the death of our child, and then I left her." He sighed.

"I'm so sorry. Do you want to cross into the light or stay here?" I asked them.

They looked at each other for confirmation. *"We would like to stay here if that's okay with everyone,"* William responded.

"It's alright; I'm sure everyone will agree as long as you're happy; that's all that matters," I told them.

They smiled at me, and holding hands, they disappeared through the wall.

"So, what's happening?" Christina asked.

"William brought his girlfriend Sarah here to meet me. She died a few years after he did. She lost their baby, then William died, and she never recovered. She died five years after William. They want to remain here; there are a lot of good memories here for them both." I explained to them.

Our dinners arrived, and the conversation turned to the upcoming investigations at the Commodore and Norblad hotels.

The investigation of the hotels was scheduled for Saturday night. One-half of the group would investigate the Commodore, and the other half would investigate the Norblad Hotel. Each group would spend a few hours at the respective hotels and trade places. We would meet up the following morning for breakfast and have a roundtable discussion.

Our first investigation would take place at the Norblad Hotel. Wendy and I left our hotel to meet the others in the basement of the Norblad hotel. Parking the car, we walked to the Norblad. We noticed someone leaving the hotel and realized it was Stuart coming out of the door and he didn't look good.

"I was just attacked by a demon; it felt like it was trying to rip my spine out. I had to get out of there."

"Here, turn around so I can heal your spine and take the pain away," I told him. Years ago, I found out I had the gift of laying on of hands as an angelic being. I had done this for him before, so I reached out and took the pain away.

"That's better, thank you." He said after the healing.

"Are you up to coming back inside with us, or do you need a few minutes? You know you can't show these things any weakness because if you do, they'll return." I reminded him.

"Yeah, just give me a couple of minutes, and I'll come in; you go ahead, I'll be all right." He assured me.

Wendy and I went into the hotel and headed downstairs to the basement. I could feel the presence of an old demon waiting for me in the basement. I turned to Wendy and said, "Protect yourself; the old one isn't happy I'm here."

Entering the basement, I saw Christina sitting in the chair, watching the others with their EMF detectors and cameras.

"You saw Stuart. Is he doing all right?" Christine asked me urgently.

"Yes, he's fine. I did a healing on him, so his pain is better. The negative is over in the corner, watching and waiting for me." I told her matter-of-factly.

"Yeah, I could feel something dark when I came down here. Once I knew it was here, I wanted to go outside and wait for you to come. But Stuart wouldn't have it; he wanted to face this thing. Sometimes, he's just too stubborn for his own good."

"He was right to face it but tried to face it alone; he should've waited for me. Together, we are stronger." I told her.

I could feel the shift in energy as the demon moved out of the corner, shifting to the left and watching everyone; it seemed curious about what we were doing. I heard the door open behind me and turned to see Stuart entering the basement.

"How are you feeling now?" Christina asked her husband.

"Better, much better. Don't worry, I'll be all right; let's get to this." He told his wife, kissing her.

I looked at him and said, "We need to split up and monitor the demon from all angles. Wendy and I will go to the right, and Stuart, you, and Christina will go to the left side of the basement. This way will be able to watch its movements closely. It's on the move, watching what we're doing. We amuse it; it thinks no one can see it, so it can move among us without being detected. It's a very old nasty demon and, of course, Is accompanied by the proverbial creepy crawlies running around." I told him.

"Well, it wasn't one of the little guys who attacked me. I would bet good money that it was the old one that attacked me." Stuart said grimly.

"Oh, course it was, it thinks were all stupid and weak. As usual, it only looks at the outside and never past the surface. I think it's time we did a little watching of our own." I told him, smiling. "I want you to head over to the left side and watch. You should be able to feel it if it comes close to you or if it changes direction. If it changes direction, get out of its way. Start saying prayers and keep your guard up." I activated the recording app on my Cell Phone. We were doing this so I could see what I could pick up later.

"I'm getting a little activity over here," Wendy said softly, chuckling, "someone or something is trying to pull the top of my boot down."

I headed straight for the far end of the basement. I stayed in that area for a few minutes, watching the negative entities but not acknowledging them. It had been observing us, now it was my turn to observe them. It only took me a few minutes to realize There had to be a portal somewhere; these old ones didn't just walk into our world; there had to be a door somewhere.

Closing my eyes, I brought Auriel forward and examined the room through angelic eyes. I could see an opening in the wall on the far-left side of the basement. It was a dark portal, and it needed to be closed before I could take care of removing the negatives. I had to cut off their escape route. Christina and Stuart were standing a short distance away from it. I signaled them to come towards me. I couldn't close it with them standing right next to it. Wendy was over to my right; I could tell she was also sensing something.

Turning toward the portal I concentrated on closing the opening while the negatives were distracted. Once the portal was closed, I turned my attention to the old negative. I caught Wendy's eye and signaled to let her know I was about to do the removal.

Auriel grabbed the old demon by the throat and examined it.

"I know you; you are Te*****. I wouldn't have considered these mortals worth your time or energy." Auriel told him curiously.

"You have no business interfering with us; we have no quarrel with you! Why do you care? I know you have no love for these mortals?" It screeched at her.

"Interesting, it must be the minister you are after. Well, the minister is a friend of mine and under my protection, so that makes it my business. I've closed your portal, so there is only one way out." Auriel said, smiling with glee.

Holding out her hand she created an infinity orb and proceeded to stuff the demon and the rest of its henchmen into the orb. Releasing the orb, it fell into the dark realm. Once that was done Auriel retreated back into my consciousness.

I closed my eyes and focused on the physical world events. Opening my eyes, I noticed everyone was looking at me as if I had grown a second head or something.

"What's wrong? Is my hair sticking up or something?" I asked, laughing.

Christina was the first to answer, "No, it's just that it never ceases to amaze me every time Auriel comes out. It blows me away when your eyes turn white, and you look like you're about twenty-five.?" She said shaking her head. "What does it feel like when it happens?

I had to stop and think about it, I had become so used to it that it took me a moment to try to get the right words to explain it.

"People often ask me what it feels like when Auriel comes forward. This is what it feels like: My consciousness steps backward and watches from a distance when she comes forward. I can hear, see, feel, and sense everything she does. Once she senses the negatives, it's like a fire filling my body, and with the fire comes a rush of pure power, white-hot and all-consuming. She focuses completely on anything negative in her path during the removal process. Her only thought is to destroy the negative, but sometimes she is restrained from killing them. She cannot take the law into her own hands, so to speak; she kills those who have brought pain and suffering to humans. All the others have to be sent back into the dark realm." I explained.

"That's got to be draining on you physically, mentally, and emotionally," Stuart observed.

"Mostly, it depends on what type and how many I am dealing with. The stronger the demon, the more power it takes; if there are many of them, it takes a toll. The old ones like this one are very draining; it will probably take me a few days to regain my energy." I told him.

"So, types of negatives, were they?" Christina asked.

"There was a dark portal that had to be closed first so they couldn't escape. Then there was an old demon named Te*****, whom Auriel had dealt with before, and six creepy crawlies. She stuffed them all in an infinity orb and returned them where they belong."

"How do you feel honey?" Wendy asked me with a look of concern on her face.

"Well, I could certainly use a large cup of coffee or a stiff drink," I said, laughing.

Everyone laughed and decided we needed to go somewhere and get a drink, then off to bed.

CHAPTER SEVEN

DEVIL CIRCLE

I received an email from a woman in Tigard, Oregon. She wrote that she and her family were seeing black shadow figures, and two of her animals were found dead. She lived with her husband, two daughters, one of whom was autistic, and her mother.

This was an urgent situation for me, and I called her immediately. I planned to visit her home the following weekend.

I called my para-partner, Wendy, and filled her in on the details.

"So, can you go with me this weekend, or do you have something planned? Don't worry if you can't go; I can handle it alone." I reassured her.

I had been doing removals for years before I took on a partner, but she enjoyed going with me on these cases. It's always a learning experience for her; sometimes, you run into things you have never encountered before.

"It didn't matter if I did have something; I would cancel because littles (children) come first. And I know for you the animals come first." She said, and I could hear the smile in her voice.

"Okay, I have the address, and we'll go on Saturday around 10 am. I'll let you drive as you know that area better than I do."

"Alright, I'll pick you up a little after nine, and we'll head out."

The evening before the removal, I was driving home from work and got a call from my son. We were in the middle of the conversation when my son's voice disappeared, and I could hear a loud, nasty growl. Then the same deep nasty voice told me: "Stay away bitch; you cannot help them, and more will die because of your interference." Then the line cleared, and I could hear my son frantically calling my name.

"Mom, Mom, are you okay? What the hell was that? It didn't sound good."

"Nothing to worry about, just a very nasty demon warning me off of the removal I'm going to do tomorrow," I told him casually.

"I don't like it; what if it hurts you? Maybe you shouldn't go!"

"You don't have to worry about me getting hurt; remember what Michael said? He protects my physical body. He won't let anything happen to me or my family." I tried to reassure him.

"Okay, but I still don't like it; I'll ask Gabriel to help you too."

I hung up the phone sending a telepathic message to Gabe to have him watch over my family while I take care of the nasty demon.

Arriving home, I packed the things I needed for the removal into my case. The items included holy water, anointing oil, black salt, sage, and instructions for laying down the black salt.

Before bed, I prayed and spoke with the legion and God. It is always how I begin to prepare for the success of the removal.

The morning of the removal dawned overcast and grey, a perfect setting for what I would do. I had breakfast with my husband at a local café and filled up on coffee. We discussed the usual things: work, weather, and the upcoming week. My husband never asked me about removals. I asked him once why he never asked, and here's what he told me:

"I figure you know what you're doing, and me just asking questions would be a distraction for you when that is the last thing you need."

He was right; his questions would only lead to him worrying about me and my actions.

Wendy arrived at nine with a cup of hot coffee for me. "Thanks for the coffee. I really need it." I told her.

"I knew you needed it; you always do. So, can you pick up on what's waiting for us?" She asked.

"It's an old nasty demon, and it was summoned, so that means someone has been doing satanic rituals by the house. I think there's a wooded area nearby; that's where they were done. Something about the backyard, what's up with the backyard?" I said, trying to work out the information I was receiving.

I could feel the negative entity trying to block me from discovering anything more about the situation. I smiled, knowing that the closer I got to the location, the more information I would get, and the negative wouldn't be able to block me.

Looking at me, Wendy asked, "Okay, what's that little smile all about?"

"The negative is trying to block me, not a very intelligent move," I told her, laughing.

The conversation turned to mundane everyday things, such as work and home. About a block away from our destination I could feel the demon trying to reach out to squeeze the air from my lungs. I blocked its attempts and it tried to lash out again but was frustrated when it couldn't affect me.

"Wow, my head just exploded," she said, glancing at me with a question.

"Yeah, it's trying to reach out and stop us from coming," I confirmed ruefully.

As we pulled up in front of the house, I noticed a wooded area behind it. I knew instinctively this was the place where the rituals were done.

Getting out of the car, I grabbed my bag with the things I would need to remove, clear the home, land, and place a protective barrier down around the home. When I placed a foot on the property, I could see, hear, and feel the negatives milling around. I completely ignored them and made my way to the front door. Before we could knock on the door, it swung open.

A middle-aged woman opened the door, motioning us to come inside. I let Wendy go first, as she was the more diplomatic of us. "Hello, I'm Jenna, are you June," she asked Wendy.

"No, this is June." She said, pointing towards me.

We entered the living room, and I saw a black mass sitting in the corner of the ceiling above the wood stove. Most people would have brushed it off as soot from the stove, but if you watched it carefully, you could see it move ever so slightly. It was a negative entity trying to escape detection. I noted it but did not address the issue; I had bigger fish to fry.

We sat on the couch, and I half listened to the woman tell Wendy what had happened in the house for several months.

"I grew up in this house, it's my mother's home. Until a few months ago, there was no paranormal activity in or near the house. There is a wooded area behind the house, which used to be owned by an older woman. I remember her telling us as kids not to go into the woods behind the house as strange things happened there, and it wasn't safe for us to play there. We never went into the woods; sometimes we would hear strange noises coming from the woods." Jenna told us.

I stood up and casually moved toward the other side of the living room bordering the backyard. I could feel a powerful dark energy coming from the area behind the house.

"What sort of activity are you experiencing?" Wendy asked.

"My daughter's pet rat was found with her neck broken. The rat's head had been pulled through the bars of the cage which were less than a half inch wide. We found our parrot dead when we got up in the morning, its head had been twisted off. Something has been trying to attack my mother's dog, and my mom's health is suddenly failing; she was fine before all of this started." Jenna said, a tremor in her voice. I could tell she was on the verge of tears.

"Excuse me, can we go into the backyard? I think there's a dark portal out there," I said quietly.

"Uh, yeah, sure." She stood and approached a small door between the dining and living rooms. The door opened onto a small, enclosed porch. Opening the outer door, I could feel the energy hit me; it was like walking into a brick wall.

As I stepped into the fenced backyard, I could see a circle in my mind's eye and a pentagram with a symbol in the circle. I estimated the circle's size as about 8 feet in diameter. I could not physically see a circle and pentagram, but psychically and energetically, I could see it. Wendy followed me out into the backyard and headed for the far side of the circle, standing to face me.

Jenna followed us and said, "You're standing about where there used to be a huge circle and pentagram drawn a couple of months ago; it's been washed away by the rain. We woke up one morning to find it in the backyard, which freaked us out. For several years, we've heard something that sounded like chanting coming from the wooded area behind the house. It happens several times a year."

"I can see it in my mind's eye; Wendy is standing about where the other side of the circle is."

"You can see them, can't you?" Jenna asked, looking at my face.

"I see them in their true form; Wendy sees a shimmery disturbance," I explained.

"I can see what happened here; I can hear the chanting. The ritual was done to open a dark portal to let demons into our world. There are several of them here now, and I need to eliminate them. Please go back in the house and wait until we come back inside. It would be too dangerous for you to stay out here. I cannot protect you and remove the demons at the same time." I told her in all seriousness.

She returned to the house, and the minute the door closed behind her, all hell broke loose. I could see several entities coming out of the portal left open by those who had created it. Making the telepathic connection with the Legion of Light, They appeared in my mind's eye, surrounding the edges of the circle.

"Are you ready?" Michael asked. I could see him standing on the right side of Wendy.

Gabriel stood on the left side of the circle, and Rafael was on the right side of the circle.

"We need to get started if everyone is ready," Auriel told them. They all nodded in response as another wave of negatives came through the portal opening.

Wendy left where she was standing to follow a couple of creepy crawlies headed around the side of the house.

"She is otherwise occupied and out of harm's way," Gabriel said, indicating he had purposefully sent her away from the apex of the problem.

"Begin!" Auriel said.

Each Archangel stretched out their arms and began closing the portal. It seemed like it took an hour, but it only took a few moments.

Once the portal was closed, we refocused on the lesser demons trying to escape us. There were several of them present, with more coming from the surrounding area. I grabbed the one nearest me by the throat, and it screamed at me.

"We were summoned; you have no right to return us to the dark realm."

"It does not matter to me whether you were summoned; you have no right to be in the physical world. The foolish mortals who summoned you will pay for this!" Auriel told it with relish.

Each of the archangels grabbed a lesser demon and some of the creepy crawlies sending them back into the darkness. It took several minutes to complete the removal, leaving my physical body tired.

"It is done," Michael said, and the other archangels disappeared.

Wendy returned to where I stood and said, "That's odd. It's almost like the little creepy things just dissolved. I was following a couple of them through the side yard." She said, a questioning look on her face.

"Not to worry, I invited the Legion before we came here, and we took care of it," I told her.

"So, when were you going to tell me you invited them?" She asked, laughing.

"Well, I didn't want to worry you; I knew there were several lesser demons here and a huge dark portal. You've never been in a situation like this, and I didn't want you to get hurt, either." I explained to her.

Returning to the house, we noticed the black mass above the wood stove had disappeared. We found the family gathered in the living room.

"Everything has been removed, and the portal has been closed. You now need to lay down a line of black salt around your home to seal it from any more negative entities." I told Jenna, pulling a bag of black salt out of my valise and a paper of written instructions on laying it down. "You'll have to sage the house first and lay down the salt immediately. If you wait, something may return, and we can't have that."

"I promise I'll lay it down immediately after I sage," Jenna promised.

"Keep in touch with us and let us know how it goes," Wendy told Jenna.

"I certainly will keep in touch." She confirmed.

Before I left, I gave her a couple of my cards and told her to call me if you have any more issues.

HAUNTED MUSEUM

2017, I was busy working on a new book in my home office. When Archangel Michael dropped in for a visit

"How's the new book coming?" He asked.

"It's going, you know how it is when I'm writing, it flows, and then I realize I've been sitting for a couple of hours. If I sit too long, I get a bit stiff. So, what's up? You don't just drop into the physical world for no reason?"

"We have a new assignment for you."

"Okay, what is the assignment? I assume it's to do with a negative removal, but you usually don't appear in the physical world unless it's something big." I told him.

"You're right; it is important. God has made this a priority. This cannot wait, and you must physically go to the location."

"It must be pretty bad if I have to go there physically. So, where am I going?"

"Vegas, sin city, as I believe you call it." He said with relish.

"Vegas! You know I hate Vegas, all that human negative energy."

"I understand, but this is important. We have had the Weasel, as you call him, ferreting out. Dark sympathizers. We knew some had questionable interactions with the dark ones. We suspected there was someone leaking information to them. Many of the negative incursions we have been dealing with lately seem to have advanced knowledge of where we will strike." He said grimly. "E**** is the one we have been seeking, but we know there are more of them; it's just a matter of ferreting them out. E**** has access to inside information and must be dealt with." Michael said, steel evident in his voice.

I could feel Michael's anger simmering just below the surface. The traitor was one of the upper echelons, and it was an insult to not only himself but to all of the archangels, God, and Jesus.

"So, can you give me more information on what's happening in Vegas?" I asked.

"Weasel has discovered that a couple of the old demons have been influencing certain humans. These humans all have one thing in common: they all have physical objects with de-monic attachments. Over the years, some warrior angels who have taken human form have encoun-tered old demons. The warriors who could not destroy the demons while in physical form bound them to objects. The objects were then hidden or given to the care of another warrior angel to guard. Slowly, over the years, the dark ones have uncovered the location of these objects."

"I assume you have been monitoring the situation," I stated.

"Yes, we have been watching to see what they are planning. We knew they had a plan; we didn't know what it was. Over the past few years, have we figured out what they were planning." He explained.

"Come on, don't keep me in suspense; what are they planning?" I asked curiously.

"They have been influencing humans, leading them to the locations of these objects. Once enough of these objects were collected, they needed to find a centralized location to bring them together.

"Don't tell me, let me guess, Vegas?"

"Yes, your favorite place, but there is a bonus for you." He said, smiling.

"Uh oh, I don't think I'll like the answer, but I'll ask the question anyway. What is the bonus besides killing demons?" I asked cautiously.

"You get to visit a museum full of oddities and haunted objects!"

"Oh no, you wouldn't send me there, would you? That's mean, these types of people drive me crazy."

"You need to think about those under attack in the museum; they need your help, to say nothing of the people who visit the place." He admonished me.

"Alight, I get it. I'm being selfish. So, what are the demons trying to do with all of these old demons, set them free?" I asked curiously.

"It's much more than that. They are planning on releasing them so that they can help them open a huge dark portal and bring hundreds of thousands of demons into the physical world. Their goal is the possession and control of millions of humans to destroy the human race! This is why the trip is so important; you must be physically present to ensure all the demons attached to the objects are destroyed before they can be set free!" he informed me through clenched teeth.

"Now I see why it's so important. I will need to be able to get inside the Museum, so that means I'll have to buy tickets. You'll owe me for this one, Michael." I told him, laughing.

"Call Wendy and see if she wants to go with you. It will be fun for you both."

'I'll need to see if I can get my timeshare down there. Suzy lives in Reno; I'll see if she wants to go with us. I know I have a timeshare in Reno. We can stay overnight in Reno, pick up Suzy, and head to Vegas." I mused to myself, already planning the trip in my mind.

Michael laughed hardily, "I can see you are already making plans, but don't forget to have some fun on your trip. You can even swing by area 51." He teased, disappearing.

I called my friend Wendy and let her know about my visit with Michael; she was excited to do the road trip and said she would call Suzy to see if she would like to go.

A week later I had booked my timeshare in Reno and Las Vegas for the trip and bought tickets online for the walk through the Museum.

We drove through Reno, Nevada, and checked into the timeshare, where we both collapsed for the next couple of hours before heading for the pool and a relaxing soak. We ordered dinner and vegged out for the evening.

Early the next morning, we headed to Suzy's house on the city's outskirts. Loading up Suzy's things, we got in the car and started the long trek to Las Vegas. Michael was right; our route took us to the fabled Area 51 site. Seven hours later, we arrived in Las Vegas and found the timeshare. Unloading the car, we all changed and headed for one of the four hot tubs. We soaked in the tub for almost an hour and found a small local restaurant for dinner.

Sitting at the restaurant table, we discussed the situation at the Haunted Museum.

"Well, here is the situation:

"I am here because a few old demons have hatched a plan to open a huge dark portal in the physical world. Lucifer's second in command, E******, is the brains behind this whole scheme. He has spearheaded the plan to bring all haunted objects with old demons to this spot. E****** has been planning this for some time."

"What do they hope to achieve by bringing all these objects together?" Suzy asked.

"I don't get it. Are they trying to release the demons attached to these objects? And just how do they think they will be able to accomplish it? They have no way of releasing their buddies. Even if you destroy the object, the demons would still be bound to whatever residual was left." Wendy asked.

"So, you know who the owner of this Museum is, right? He thinks he's got it made, all of these people bringing him objects they want to get rid of. He is essentially getting these objects for free or on loan. He doesn't know why he's getting all these demon-infested objects. He's just so self-involved that he believes this is all good luck. He has no idea what is happening and doesn't care either."

"So, what is the real reason all these people are bringing him objects?" Suzy asked.

"So, here's what's going on E*****has been influencing people with these objects to bring them to this Museum. Once there, in the location, he will open a huge dark portal once the portal is open. He and several other old demons will go through the portal into the physical world and physically release these demons, which are bound to the objects. Once that's done, he and the demons he released will bring you even more demons into the physical world. Their ultimate goal is to destroy mankind on a global scale. They can send an army into the physical world by opening this large portal."

"Holy crap, no wonder the Legion wanted you to be here in person. What does Lucifer think of this? Does he even know about it?" Wendy asked.

"Lucifer didn't know anything about it, and he's unhappy. He came to Auriel asking for a favor. He wanted her to take out his second in command. He can't do it himself because that would cause many problems. If Auriel were to take him out, then it's nothing to do with him, and no one would be any the wiser."

"Well, that's one way to look at it. You're killing two birds with one stone, and Lucifer will owe you a favor." Suzy said, laughing.

"But here's the cherry on top of the cake. A sympathizer in the light realm has been feeding the dark ones information. It's not often that we find one of our own has been working against us. For that, he must pay the ultimate price." I told them.

Keep The look on their faces was one of stunned disbelief.

"It never even occurred to me that something like this could happen," Suzy exclaimed.

"Yes, I understand; we are raised to believe everything in the light is perfect. But I can tell you for a fact that it's not. I've seen too much in this lifetime not to understand." I said, sighing heavily.

"So, did they give you any idea who the sympathizer was?" Wendy asked.

"Yes, his name is Zazial; he is one of the older archangels who is privy to much inside information. He was feeding information to Lucifer's second-in-command. Lucifer came to Auriel about the betrayal of Zazial and E****. Lucifer felt this betrayed the Legion and all they stood for. He takes this very seriously; he will not tolerate any betrayal." I told them.

"So how will you clear the demons out of the Museum? You know the Museum is going to be packed full of people. Maybe we can find a quiet corner somewhere, and you can do it?" Wendy suggested.

"We are scheduled to go through the Museum tomorrow afternoon. I think what I'm going to do is do the removal from the outside of the building. It's the only way that I can do it without anyone being harmed in the process. I won't know the full extent of the situation until we get there. The Legion will also be here; everyone is preparing for the battle. Legions of archangels and warrior angels will take part in the battle."

"Wow, the energy of that many angels will be off the chart!" Wendy commented.

We spent the day sightseeing and just taking things easy, catching up on the happenings in our lives. The weather was perfect in the 90's.

I was awoken by Archangel Micheal giving me an update on the situation at the Haunted Museum.

"We are prepared for the battle. We know over two thousand demons are amassing in the dark realm. They are awaiting the opening of the portal to enter your world. The Weasel has been monitoring the situation and keeping us apprised of their movements.”

"All right, I will prepare for the upcoming battle and put my protection in place. I will help the others to create their protection.”

Getting out of bed, I went to the kitchen and brewed a pot of coffee. The others groggily entered the kitchen, lured by the smell of brewing coffee.

"Morning, coffees done. I left you enough for one cup each.” I told them, smiling. "I need at least two cups to get myself up and running for what's to come.”

"I need some breakfast before we go to the Museum. I'm going to take a quick shower, then get dressed.” Wendy commented.

"I second that,” Suzy agreed.

Okay, you two get your shower then I'll get mine. I need to see what I can pick up about the Museum and its surroundings.”

Grabbing my coffee, I headed into my bedroom for some quiet to 'see' what was happening at the Museum and the buildings surrounding it.

Laying on the bed, I connected with Auriel and merged with her consciousness. I could see the Museum inside and several objects with demonic attachments and their location in the building. Turning to look at the buildings near the Museum I could see a group of demons in a building next to the Museum. These other buildings would also have to be cleared; we would need a couple of archangel battalions to ring both buildings' perimeters. This way, we could make certain that none of the demons escaped.

The destruction of the demons and the dark portal would have to be swift and deadly to ensure that none of the demons survived the assault. I decided not to relate what I had to the others so that none of the demons could look into their minds.

We found a small local restaurant where we stopped for breakfast and several more cups of coffee. We discussed what I had found when I did the remote viewing session.

"Well, here is what I saw: there is a Masonic lodge next to the museum and the land beneath it is infested with negative entities gathering for the opening of the dark portal. These will have to be dealt with along with the museum."

"Holy crap, how come we're just finding this out? I was under the impression it was only the museum!" Wendy said, almost at a loss for words.

"It's a good thing you checked it out!" Suzy commented.

"Yeah, I hate surprises, especially unpleasant ones. There were a lot of people lined up outside the place yesterday. I won't be able to go inside and do the removal. I'll have to do it from the outside of the building." I informed them.

"That's crazy. Don't you have to see the inside to do the removal? How do you know what's there and where it is?" Suzy asked curiously.

"I connect with Auriel and see through her eyes as the battle begins. She already knows what and who is there, so I also know."

"Wow, that's so interesting," Suzy said.

"So what exactly is there?" Wendy asked.

"Ten old demons are attached to various things and human spirits that must be released. One of the human spirits is John Wayne Gasy, the serial killer. Lucifer's (L) first in command, S******, is the mastermind behind the opening of this huge dark portal. This is a means to an end for L, his first in command has been causing distention between him and some of the other older demons. So taking him and those following him out is a win-win situation."

"Wow, I had no idea there are so many old demons attached to things there. How are we going to know that you got everything?" Suzy questioned.

"We won't stop until everything has been found and eliminated. There is also the issue of the sympathizer, who needs to be eliminated. Auriel will have to take care of him as well. He isn't aware that we know of his involvement in the situation, which gives us the advantage." I told them. "This is all I can say for now because, as they say, 'walls have ears.'

Finishing our coffee, we gathered our things and headed for the museum. We arrived at the museum at 11 am; the line was around fifty people long.

"I knew it would be a zoo!" I told them. "I am going to step out of the car to do this. I don't want either of you in the line of fire, so to speak."

Getting out of the car. I moved towards the curb where I could stand unnoticed and interrupted by a passerby. Facing the house, which passed for a museum. I closed my eyes and cleared my mind. I connected with Auriel and merged my consciousness with hers.

In my mind's eye, I could see the museum inside the room where the debit box resided. I could see L's first in command, S******. Auriel cloaked herself to remain unseen. That way, she could observe what was happening without the dark one knowing she was there. On the other side of where they would open the portal, S****** and three other old demons and a group of about a thousand old demons, were gathered. As I listened to them, I could hear them planning what they would do once the portal was open. S****** would come through first and release the old demons from their bondage to the physical world objects. He reasoned that they would be so grateful to him for releasing them that they would align with his plans.

Once released, they would open the dark portal and let S******'s followers into the physical world. He intended to have each old demon loyal to him attach themselves to humans in places of power worldwide. Several hundred of them were already attached to people with power and influence. He was not satisfied with that. He wanted every powerful and influential person to be influenced by him to destroy the world. They would start with finances and spirituality, two major factors in destroying mankind.

This would cause worldwide chaos, depression, anger, and violence, which would ultimately lead to a world war that would destroy everyone and everything. Bringing with it chaos and enabling the darkones to have dominion over mankind.

Auriel decided that we should probe deeper into S******'s mind to find out more about who, if anyone had authorized this action.

It's never pleasant to go into the mind of a demon. There is such chaos, hatred, and anger that there is room for nothing else. You always come out feeling like you will never be clean again. The sensation wears off after a few minutes, but it still is something I don't particularly like doing, but it is sometimes necessary.

Auriel and I pushed our way into its mind. I searched for the memory of where this plan all began. It seemed to be just out of reach, so we pushed even deeper. We finally found the memory we were searching for. It turns out that L was unaware of this plan. We also found out it intended to kill Lucifer and take over the dark realm after successfully transitioning his followers into the physical world.

Auriel never liked L's first in command; she didn't trust him and knew he would try to take over L's position if there was a way. This situation seemed to validate her assessment of his character.

Pulling out of its mind, we saw the four old demons begin to create the dark portal opening. Auriel connected with the archangel Michael telepathically:

"It has begun. Is everyone in place?"

"Yes, we are ready." He responded.

The Legion appeared cloaked next to where the portal was beginning to form. Watching for the first sign of their intrusion into the physical world.

The three old demons Auriel and I saw came through the opening along with S******. As they came through, the Legion uncloaked, and the battle began.

More demons pushed through the portal, but the Legion had already foreseen the possibility; three battalions of archangels met them as they came through the portal.

The battle continued until the surge of incoming demons dwindled to nothing. S****** was captured, and the portal was held open for one last task.

The archangels Gabriel and Raphael held S****** securely.

"You have been found guilty of incursion into the physical world with the intention of the destruction of mankind," Micheal pronounced. "The judgment for your crime is death!"

"You have no dominion over me or the dark realm! Only Lucifer can pass judgment on me, and he sanctioned this!"

"I have looked into your mind and discovered that L had nothing to do with this! I also confirmed it with him myself." Auriel responded, smiling secretly.

In one swift movement, she pulled a dagger out of her belt and sunk it into the heart of the demon. Once the dagger had found its mark, I could see a bolt of white light energy shoot straight into heaven. The bolt found its mark, striking the heavenly sympathizer E**** and killing him.

Pulling the dagger out of S******'s chest, he exploded into harmless molecules that drifted into space.

"All of the negatives have been eliminated. There were no survivors or escapees!" Michael related the status of the battle.

"Now we kill the demons attached to the physical objects," Auriel said succulently.

Each archangel picked an object and released the demon, killing it as it was separated from the object.

"It is done; none are left," Raphael informed Michael.

Looking at Auriel, Michael told her, "You did well; it's time for you to return to your physical body."

"Yes, it was great fun, as usual!" she laughed.

I could feel my consciousness returning to my body. I staggered back to the car, climbing into the passenger seat, exhausted from the battle.

"Well, has it been cleared out?" Wendy asked, looking at me with concern. "You look like you've just run a marathon."

"Yes, it's clear, but I think we need to do the tour to ensure we didn't miss anything if you know what I mean," I told her.

Wendy parked the car, and we took our place in the line of people waiting to enter the museum. It took us another forty-five minutes to reach the front of the line. Waiting for our turn a man dressed in a shirt marked security came out of a side entrance. He approached the woman, letting people into the museum, and as he spoke to her, she left, and he seemed to be taking over her station. As we got to the front of the line, he seemed to be staring intently at me.

"Hey, I know you, you're the demon seer! I worked security with the camera crew when you were on the show!"

"Yeah, that's me. How are you?" I acknowledged.

"What are you doing here?" he asked.

"Taking care of business," I told him meaningfully.

He just grinned and shook his head as he opened the door and motioned me in.

The three of us entered the museum and walked through the entire exhibit. Opening myself up, I could not detect any negative entities present.

Leaving the building, we looked at each other and headed to the car.

"Well, I certainly couldn't feel anything bad in there," Wendy commented.

"Me either." Suzy agreed, "what about you?" she said, looking at me.

"Nope, nothing left. But I wonder how long it will last, knowing the owner?" I commented.

We arrived back at the timeshare in record time.

"I don't know about anyone else, but I'm ready for the hot tub I saw by the pool," Wendy commented.

"You bet I am more than ready!" I agreed.

"Me too; let's bring the wine," Suzy suggested.

We all laughed and headed for the room to change into our swimsuits.

Grabbing towels, three glasses, and a bottle of wine, we headed for the empty hot tub to relax.

We spent another day in Las Vegas before heading home through Reno to drop off Suzy.

The trip was one we would all not soon forget.

CHAPTER NINE

REVENGE

It was the middle of August when I received an email from my friend Bruce. He said he was visiting a friend doing energy healing on him when he got there; she told him that she was given a message for him. She told him there was an ancient negative entity, an enemy of the light. It was searching for someone in the physical world with an archangel or a warrior angel within them. They say you know this person. The ancient being is the one who has been sending all manner of negatives after him. This enemy was very powerful, but an entity of light would come forth and defeat it.

"She will kill the enemy and end his rampage in our world. She will succeed. I heard "ferocious," relentless but tired. But also feels like she is getting briefings from above. She and Michael seem to be connected, intertwined! She is by no means alone in this (I'm hearing). Overwhelming show of force by the good side. 'It will be done'. They want it done."

"I heard they are prepared for battle. They have a secret weapon (up their sleeve) that they don't know about, can't see (haven't seen?). The enemy is not prepared for whatever this weapon is. The dark ones believe they are going to win -- but the light says the other side is overplaying their hand, and they don't know what they are in for. I'm told this person is a fierce battle-tress. A force to be reckoned with. Oh my. She has quite the reputation, this is wonderful."

"The main thing is they have something in store for the dark ones that they believe will be lethal. That is their belief. The angel they sent to relay this message showed herself. She's wonderful, can I keep her? She's no slouch! I wrote down her name, Sephora. I think I spelled it correctly." She finished relaying the message.

He had a lot to think over, and when he arrived home, an angel whispered in his ear, "The light shall defeat the darkness." then he was given a vision; he sent an email recounting his vision and the message to me:

"Auriel, the archangel on a hill, mounted on a winged horse with four other archangels behind her, all with swords, shields, and body armor. The swords and armor were silver; they glowed and appeared made from white light energy. The archangels included Michael, Raphael, Gabriel, and Auriel. Behind the four was an army of angels standing at the ready."

"I'm standing on a hill, and below the hill on flat land stood M*****, the son of Lucifer. Behind him, a legion of demons awaited his command. Then, I find myself standing between the two armies on the left side of the battlefield. I watched Auriel touch her horse's flank and charge towards M****** with the other Archangels following closely behind her."

"As I watched, I could see the two sides clashing; the fierceness of the battle was like nothing I had ever seen. Auriel was a powerful force to be reckoned with. The archangel's swords drew blood again and again, killing hundreds of demons. Finally, Auriel was able to get to M******; with one powerful swing of her sword, she sliced off his head, and he virtually disintegrated. What was left of his army retreated into nothingness, and the vision disappeared." He said, seemingly still amazed at what he saw.

I told him I had a similar vision a couple of days before the email from him but said nothing to him as I did not want to upset him.

I called him and explained what was happening:

"The reason you've been having so many negative things going on in your life is because M****** is using you to get to me. He knew Auriel had been reborn but didn't know which vessel (body) she was inhabiting. He's been searching for over two hundred years.

Remember, it's a chess game between the dark and light; we, like many others, are pawns. The demons Auriel had been removing were collateral damage as far as he was concerned, and he used them to find her.

M******** sent a message to Auriel to challenge her to a battle. Auriel said she would do battle when it suited her and chose 8-18-18. She let me know that I would need to be in a quiet place and lay down as she would leave my body completely to do battle.

The moment arrived, and I called Bruce to let him know it was time and asked him to link with me so he could see what was happening.

I informed Bruce: *"Lucifer came to me; he does not approve of what his son is doing; I asked him about it. He says, 'I do not sanction it. It is not how we do things; he will pay the price for it himself I will not help him!' Lucifer does not have his back and he is doomed to failure because of it. Auriel is out in front because this was a direct challenge from Lucifer's son M******."*

My consciousness would be there as a part of Auriel. I didn't know how long the battle would last, but I asked my son to keep the dogs quiet until I was through. Closing my eyes, I went into an altered state, and the battle began…

Both warring sides were arrayed in armor. The archangel's armor looked like a shining silver armor reflecting the power of white light.

Their swords are made of pure white light energy. The Dark Ones armor looked like glowing black steel with a fiery emblem emblazoned on the chest plate.

The leaders were mounted on horses. Auriel had three archangels behind her and shadowy figures of more archangels and warrior angels behind them.

Behind M***** are a hundred lesser demons. The battle begins when Auriel lifts her sword. Both sides advancing towards each other. M****** stayed behind his army and only advanced once his warriors engaged the enemy. All the archangels fought fiercely, taking on the dark army. Swords clashing, two archangels sustained minor injuries, but they continued to fight. Twisting, turning, dodging, spinning, and slicing the forces of light destroyed the dark army down to the last demon; only the leader, M******, remained.

During the fight, I could feel Auriel's movements as if they were mine. My body jerked and spasmed with each thrust of her sword. I felt every blow she made; it was exhilarating. A burst of light shot through me, and I saw and felt God adding to Auriel's angelic power, giving me energy in the physical world.

Knowing this was Auriel's battle, the other archangels deferred to Auriel, encircling

M*****. Auriel entered the circle, her sword at the ready.

"Your forces are gone, you stand alone, no one will help you now. Even your father has forsaken you."

"I have others I can summon who will fight for me." M***** growled.

"Summon them if you dare, but they will meet the same fate as the others." She warned him. "You started this battle, and I will finish it. God has handed down your judgment, death." She told him with relish.

"No!" He lunged at her, his sword barely missing her.

She quickly countered, and they fought for several minutes until Auriel disarmed him. Grabbing him from behind, she held the sword to his throat.

"Recall your minions from the physical world; do it now!"

"I will not, not unless you promise not to kill me." his voice ringing out in anger and fear.

"I promise, and I warn you I will know if they have not been recalled." She warned him.

"I won't be held responsible for what they do on their way out of the physical world, "he warned her. He knew archangels always kept their promises and thought he was safe. He sent out a recall and told them to do as much harm as possible on the way out.

Auriel sensed his thoughts although there was not much she could do about it now.

"It's done," he told her.

She shook him viciously, "ALL OF THEM!" she said through clenched teeth. To make her point, she tightened the pressure of her sword against his throat.

"Alright, alright!" he acquiesced, feeling the sword burning his throat.

"Haniel, see what you can do; he's telling them to cause more problems as they leave," Auriel told him.

He nodded, taking half the white light army with him to mitigate as much damage as possible.

When the last minion was recalled or destroyed, Auriel fulfilled the sentence God had passed on M******.

"M******, you have instructed your followers to cause pain and suffering to innocent humans. You incited a war against me and the other archangels. You disrespected God and even your father, Lucifer, all for revenge. God has passed judgment: death." She said solemnly.

"But you promised you wouldn't kill me." His shrill screech filled the heavens as he struggled even harder.

"I promised, but I didn't say what I promised," she reminded him succulently. Drawing the sword back swiftly, it sliced his throat, scattering his energy among the stars.

With the release of the negative's energy, a flash of light lit the angelic plane, sending a surge of power through the heavens.

Auriel raised her sword, shouting, "It is done."

I could feel Auriel returning to my body; she was exhausted yet energized at the same time. I sat up and swung my legs over the side of the bed. Standing I felt a sharp pain go through my left knee. I was confused as to why it hurt then I remembered Auriel being injured in the knee during the battle. The pain lasted for a couple of days and then subsided.

"Now that M*****'s henchmen have been recalled, there is no fear of them returning because Lucifer is dealing with their betrayal, so things should start to get better now for all concerned. "Auriel informed me.

I knew that battle was over, but the war against the darkness would continue, and Auriel and I would be there.

CHAPTER TEN

SHANGHAI TUNNELS

My cell phone rang one evening and I saw by the caller ID it was Stuart.

"What's up?" I asked him.

"I'm calling to ask if you want to join my paranormal group, NW Paranormal Investigative team. I've recently had a couple of members leave the group."

I was curious as to why they had left the group but didn't ask, as I was not feeling anything negative, just some annoyance.

"How many people do you have in your group?" I asked him.

"We are down to four; people have other commitments and have had to leave the group. I recently parted ways with the co-founder of the group."

I wondered about the reason for the breakup between the co-founders but decided not to ask.

"Alright, sure," I responded.

I had been a member for a few months when I got a call from Stuart on a Monday evening.

"How are things? Can you talk or are you busy?" he asked.

"No, I can talk, what's up?"

"I started volunteering at the Shanghai Tunnels, giving tours a couple of nights a week." He informed me.

"Nice, I've never been there, but I've heard about it; supposed to be haunted."

"Yeah, it is, but here's the thing. The guy in charge of the preservation of the Tunnels keeps getting attacked and constantly getting sick. This is new; there's never been a problem before the last couple of weeks. He wants our team to go down and investigate to find out what's happening and help resolve the issue if possible. Since you've never been there before, I thought we could do a walk-through first so you can see what you can pick up."

"Okay, so when do you want to do this?" I asked him. My mind was racing to remember what I had planned for the following weekend.

"Would you be available this Friday evening to do the walk-through and see what you can pick up? We can all have dinner around seven, then do the walk-through," he asked.

"Yeah, that's fine. I have a friend who had been asking to go with me on an investigation; I know she'll want to go."

"That's cool; I'm letting some of my boys come."

"Yeah, that will work. Give me the address, and I'll be there." Write down the address.

"It's right below the Hobo's restaurant in old Chinatown in Portland. Meet us at 7 pm, and I'll get the keys if John's not there yet."

"Okay, I'll google it. See you Friday evening."

I was already getting information on what was there waiting in the tunnels, and it wasn't nice.

"*Michael*?" I summoned Michael, the archangel, telepathically.

"*I'm here, and yes, it's exactly what you are sensing: a lesser demon. It should be interesting, the perfect place for them, you know. Lots of pain and suffering went on there.*"

At work the next day, I asked Beth, who worked with me, if she wanted to go to the Shanghai tunnels.

"Hey what are you doing Friday evening?" I asked her.

"Sitting around watching the telly. Why, what's up?" she asked curiously.

"How would you like to go to the Shanghai tunnels with me? I have to do a walk-through before we do an investigation."

"Hell yeah, when do when should I be ready?"

"I'll pick you up at six and we can head down there. We're going to have dinner before the walk-through.

Friday evening I picked Beth up and we headed for Old Chinatown. Arriving in old town, the traffic was hectic, with no on-street parking available. We spent the next five minutes looking for a parking spot before settling for a pay lot.

I could feel a negative presence close by when I got out of the car. During the short three blocks walk to the restaurant, I encountered multiple entities going about their business. Arriving at the restaurant, we stepped inside, and the heaviness of the atmosphere hit me like a ton of bricks.

Stuart sat at a table with Steve Z and several of his family members.

"Stuart, this is Beth. I work with her, and she's always up for new things, so I brought her."

"Glad you both could make it." He said, hugging me. "You haven't met Adam yet; he's one of our tech guys. He can't get to very many investigations because he travels often for his job."

I shook hands with Adam, and we settled into several empty chairs. I could feel and see movement all around me. The others discussed how to get the best coverage for the investigation using static infrared cameras. I tuned them out and began speaking with the local ghosts.

"Don't go down there. It isn't safe." A young woman informed me. She looked to be Native American in her mid-twenties. *"There's a demon down there; it's best to stay away."* She warned me.

I responded telepathically, *"I know, that's why I'm here."*

"Are you crazy? That thing is nasty, and it likes to hurt people. It can kill you." She whispered.

"I came here to get rid of it for you. Do you know who I am and what I can do about it?" I asked her to see if she could see beyond the physical covering.

"You're a medium; I know that because you can see and hear me. Are you telling me you can take this thing away?" She asked in disbelief.

"Look deeper!" I advised her and brought Auriel forward.

"I see now. Forgive me, Auriel." She said, bowing slightly.

Auriel returned to the back of my consciousness. *"What is your name? Auriel is not upset; she understands your concern for the physical body. We will remove what is in the tunnels so you will no longer have to be concerned for yourself and the other souls."* I reassured her.

"My name is Niea. There is a human soul down there who is negative. In life, he shanghaied people, including women like me, who were forced into prostitution. I try to protect these tunnels against him, but he is very strong." She warned me.

"Do not be concerned about him; he will have to leave the tunnels and answer for his crimes," I reassured her.

"Hey, June, are you in there?" Stuart asked, laughing. "Where did you go? For a few minutes there, you seemed to be somewhere else."

"I was having a conversation with one of the local ghosts," I told him.

"Did they have anything interesting to say?" Beth asked.

"One of them was a native American woman. She was trying to warn me about the negative's downstairs in the tunnels. But I already knew they were there. The moment I got out of the car, I felt them." I told him.

"So, there's something negative in the tunnels? Is there a problem with the kids going down with us?" Stuart asked in concern.

"Normally, yes, but with me here, it's okay; I'll keep them safe," I assured him.

"Alright, are you ready to head downstairs to the tunnels then?" he asked.

"Yeah, I'm ready whenever you want to head down."

Entering the tunnels through an old freight elevator opening, I could feel several entities watching inside the tunnels. John, the caretaker of the tunnels, was giving us a tour, relaying the tunnels' history and the Shanghai activity in the local area. I tuned him out and opened my senses to see what was moving around me. I decided then and there not to acknowledge any spirits except the woman I met in the restaurant.

At the end of the tour, there was a walled-off area on the far side of the room where they would lock men up awaiting delivery to waiting ships. In the open area of the room, an old wooden cigar store Indian stood alone and out of place. A rough, nasty-looking male spirit stood leaning against the statue, glaring at everyone. I was so caught up in observing him that I didn't realize I had leaned back against the original brick wall structure. Once my back encountered the wall, psychometry took over. I watched as past events played in front of me like watching a video. I was experiencing all of this through my mind's eye. I also experienced all the emotions and graphic scenes that had taken place in the tunnels since its conception. Once the images stopped, I realized I was leaning against the wall.

"Hey, are you okay?" Stuart asked in concern.

I hadn't realized that Stuart had come over to me. "I'm okay. I made the mistake of leaning against the wall, and everything came rushing towards me at one time."

"You mean like psychometry?"

"Yes, exactly. That's why I usually don't handle things at a second-hand shop. Emotions and traumatic events, if they are intense enough, can be absorbed into the location itself. I think I've seen everything I need to see. I'm going to see if Beth is ready to leave." I told him.

I found Beth in the room where the tunnels started. "Are you about ready to head out?" I asked her.

"Yeah, this place gives me the creeps. I swear I heard something growl. Did they keep dogs down here?" she asked nervously.

"Uh, it wasn't a dog, you heard," I told her.

"Then hell yeah, I'm ready to go."

We said our goodbyes and headed home. On the ride home, Beth asked me. "So, if it wasn't a dog, what growled at me?"

I glanced at her and said, "A demon."

"Damn, why couldn't it have been a dog!" she commented ruefully.

We laughed and spent the rest of the drive talking about other things.

I got a call from Stuart the next day.

"So, just what did you get when you were down there?" Stuart wanted to know.

"I could feel a negative earthbound, a demon, and several other trapped souls. Someone has opened up a portal on the far side of the tunnels by doing seances and using a Ouija board. If I go down there and remove things, it had better be soon."

"I'll see how soon John can get us down there to take care of this. I want to film the removal; how do you feel about that?"

"Personally, I don't care. I will be too busy doing the removal to worry about anything else. The only day I have off during the week is Wednesday." I told him quickly, trying to remember if I had anything else scheduled.

"Awesome, the curator, John, is usually there around 11 am. Will that work for you?" Stuart asked. "Oh, and can you bring your camera for the filming?"

"Yeah, that's good. Hopefully, the traffic isn't too bad around that time."

Wednesday arrived rainy and cold. Looking out the window I sighed heavily, how I hated the cold and rain.

I left around 10 am and met the others at Hobo's restaurant.

While the others set up the equipment, I started taking pictures and tuning in on the activity. I brought some black salt, which I had recently made up.

"So, what's here?"

"There was only one negative last week now there's three. I'll need to lay down some black salt to keep everyone safe. You need to tell everyone they need to stay within the circle of salt I lay down."

"Alright, I'll do it now," Stuart said, heading towards where the others were gathered.

I grabbed my bag of salt and headed for where I knew the negatives were located. I created a black salt circle. Everyone was starting to filter in the area where I had laid the salt down.

"Can I have everyone's attention? As you can see on the ground, there is a line of black salt." I showed them.

Everyone looked at the black line visible on the ground.

"When I start to do the removal, the only safe place for you will be inside the circle. If you step outside the circle during the removal, the negatives may lash out at you, injuring you physically. It's best if you don't speak or move while I do the removal." I informed them,

"How many of them are there?" Stuart asked.

"When we first did the walk-through, there was only one of them; now there are three," I responded.

"Wow, where did the other two come from?"

"Someone opened another portal by using a Ouija board and not closing the portal afterwards. I'll close the portal first, or others will enter our world." I told him.

Heading back to a long stretch of the tunnel where pipes ran through, I could see the portal at the far end. Seeing the portal in my mind, I pictured it closing and used the angelic energy within me to seal it. I returned to the large room where the demons were located. Making sure everyone was in the black salt circle. I began the removal process.

"Everyone, please ensure you're inside the circle and remember that no matter what you see or hear, *do not leave the circle.* It's the only place where you will be protected." I warned them.

As I started the removal process, I vaguely registered a comment from behind me.

"Oh my God, was that a growl?"

"I heard it, too!" Someone else said.

The more powerful of the three demons came forward a sword clinched in each hand.

"Bitch I will kill you and torture your soul for an eternity." It snarled, moving towards me.

Auriel came forward, and I could feel her exit my body, leaving me feeling empty. I could see, feel, and hear what she was going through.

She drew her white light swords and stood squarely before the demon. "Spawn of Satan, I know you not, but you will surely not forget me! Prepare to die at the hands of Auriel, defender of the light and demon slayer." She could see her identity surprised the demon. She saw a quickly masked look of fear in the demon's eyes.

The other two demons stood back and watched the first one, and she could tell they weren't sure what the outcome would be.

"You are nothing; I will kill you without a second thought." It snarled and lunged forward.

Sword met sword in a vicious clash. Swords met repeatedly, near misses, and the demon received several wounds. The clash seemed to last forever, but it was only a matter of a minute. Disarming the demon, she grabbed it by the throat and cast it back into the dark realm. She cast an infinity orb towards the other two demons before they could react and sent them back into the darkness.

Returning to my body I felt drained yet energized at the same time. I turned back to the others only to see them all staring at the spot where the demons had come through.

"Uh, June, your eyes are strange; they look white, not blue, and your face is different. I actually saw wings coming out of your shoulders. I don't know how to explain it." Stuart said, staring in amazement.

"Really, as I don't have a mirror, I couldn't tell you what I look like. I'm told when Auriel comes out, my face, eyes, voice change, and wings come out of my shoulders." I said, shrugging.

"I've never seen anything like it. It feels lighter here now. Are the negatives gone now?" Stuart asked.

"Yes, they're gone, but they'll be back if someone doesn't stop doing séance and using Ouija boards down here," I warned him.

Since the initial removal I had to go back a second time because a portal was opened again. My friend Stuart was working doing tours and called me one night about something attacking people. I did the third removal from home. They opened a new part of the tunnel two years ago under a comedy club.

I could see a small wooden hatch on the floor of the new section that should never be opened; there is an evil that lives there. In due time, I may have to go down and remove it. I know another portal is open because I'm connected with the tunnels.

CHAPTER ELEVEN

MESSAGE FROM A DEMON

My next encounter with an old demon was a bit more interesting. I was invited to appear on Ghost Adventures because of my experiences with a demon at the Norblad hotel in Astoria, Oregon. I was there on an investigation on January 20, 2018, and had to remove a couple of demons.

Earlier, one of the producers of Ghost Adventures show had asked me to do another episode about the Cape disappointment lighthouse in Washington. I couldn't get off work to do it with only two days' notice, so I recommended my friend Wendy to do that episode.

I received a phone call from Jeff Ballenger in April 2018. He said he was told that I had removed demons from the hotel a couple of months before. He asked me if I would appear in the episode; they were filming the Norblad hostel (hotel). The phone call went something like this:

My cell phone rang, and I answered it at work.

"Hello, is this June Lundgren?" The male voice asked me.

"Yes, this is June; how can I help you?"

"Hello, my name is Jeff Ballenger. I am with the Travel Channel. I work specifically with Ghost Adventures, and I understand from my contact that you investigated the Norblad hotel a couple of months ago."

"Yes, I was there with a group of people doing paranormal investigations in three different locations one of them was the Norblad. My friend and I walked from the Commodore hotel to the Norblad Hotel. We saw our friend Stuart step out of the hotel. He didn't look too good; he told me a demon had just attacked him. I already knew there was more than one demon in the Astoria locations we were visiting." I confirmed.

"How did you know there were demons there?" As he asked the question, he heard a growl come through his phone, and then we lost contact. He called me back immediately and asked, "What was that? It sounded like a growl, and then the line went dead!" He asked almost nervously.

"Oh, it's nothing, just a demon; they don't like me talking about them," I said matter-of-factly.

"Uh, you make it sound like this is common." He commented.

"Well, it is; it's what I do; I remove demons. I'm known as a Demon Seer in Ireland, where my grandmother was from. I can see demons, understand, communicate, remove, and destroy them."

"Wow, I got your name from the guy attacked by the demon; his name is Stuart," Jeff told me.

"Yes, we are part of the same paranormal group. I had to go down and remove the demon from the basement of the Norblad hotel and close a portal that had been opened there." I told him.

"Can you come to Astoria and be available on the weekend of April 28?" He asked hopefully.

"Sure, my friend and I will come and spend the weekend. I'll have my cell phone so you can contact me through it."

"Okay, I'm not sure what time were going to be filming, but it should be on Saturday; one of the producers will call you and let you know what time it is on Saturday," Jeff told me.

What they never knew was that one month before, I was diagnosed with cancer. I was to have surgery two days before the filming of ghost adventures. My friend Wendy offered to drive me as I was not supposed to be driving then.

Wendy and I drove down to Astoria so I could recount what happened with a demonic attack in February of that year. About thirty minutes before our arrival, I received some information on what awaited me at the location.

"Hey, guess what's waiting at the hotel?" I asked my friend Wendy (co-founder of my group Ghosts and Girls Paranormal).

"Don't tell me, let me guess, a demon?" She responded with an ironic grin.

"Yup, but not just any demon, this is an Old One."

"You're kidding. I mean, they hardly ever come into the physical world, right? I've never encountered one since we've been working together." She said, awe in her voice.

"Yeah, it's one he's encountered before a few years ago," I told her.

"How do you know he's encountered it before?"

"It just told me."

"What the hell? It knows you're coming?" she asked in surprise.

"Yeah, it knows; it wants me there to give Zak a message." I sighed. "So now I'm a messenger? Geez, give me a break." I muttered more to myself than her.

"Wow, if you're in contact with it this far away, it must be pretty dam powerful." She said, considering.

"Yeah, he's been around for so long he can't even remember someone that's pissed him off as much as Zak has. He just told me that Zak has become a thorn in his side, and this will be his last warning. He said he did something to him a few years ago, but Zak didn't heed the warning."

"So, what did he do to Zak before, and where did it happen? "Wendy asked curiously.

"Don't know it wouldn't tell me and don't care. This is more conversation than I want to have with one of these Old Ones." I could hear Auriel's voice responding to her question. Suddenly, in my mind I could see Auriel fighting with the demon. The fight seemed to go on forever, but it was just a few minutes. When it finished, the demon was chained to the wall of the Norblad Hotel basement.

"Auriel just chained it to the basement wall; it's not going anywhere until she releases it," I told her grimly.

She glanced over at me with a look of surprise on her face. "I see Auriel doesn't like having a conversation with it. She's the more shoot first and ask questions later sort of a gal." She said, smiling. "This is going to be one interesting meeting; I just wish I could be there when you relay the message to Zak."

"Yeah, it should be fun to see the look on his face when I tell him." I smiled back in expectation of what was to come. "You know Zak hasn't got a clue as to what he's in for," I said seriously.

"No, I don't believe he does; I wonder how he'll take it? I only hope he doesn't blow it off. He must have really pissed this thing off. This is serious; if you piss off a demon, you pay the price." Wendy commented.

"Yeah, but that's not my problem; the old demon is my problem. It knows Auriel is coming and is willing to deal with her to get this message to Zak. It wants Auriel's assurance that she won't kill it. She has given her word, and she will keep it. We can send it back into the darkness, but you can bet it'll find a way back before too long." I told her.

"Well, we'll cross that bridge when we come to it." She responded.

"Remember what I said before? It's a chess game on the other side, and the pieces are in play. The game is two-sided with us in the middle, and it's not a situation I cherish being in." I sighed.

"Tell Auriel she needs to think about the good side in all of this. Removing an old demon that should be fun for her." Glancing at me she saw Auriel looking back at her and smiled to herself.

Arriving in Astoria the day before the filming we stayed at a local hotel. The next morning, we got up early, had breakfast with our friends, and returned to the hotel to pack our things and wait for the producer's call.

Around 10 am, I received a call from Cory Lyons, a producer, asking me to go to the Norblad Hotel at noon for the interview.

Wendy and I arrived at 11:30 and parked the car in the next block, where we had a view of the entrance to the hotel. We could see the Ghost Adventure crew coming and going between the Commodore Hotel and the Norblad. I knew that Zak was interviewing Stuart and Christina, with whom we had done the initial investigation in February. Stuart was one of the people who had been attacked by a demon when we did our investigation.

I could feel the old demon getting restless in the hotel's basement. It was struggling against the restraints Auriel had placed on him and growing impatient with Zak, wanting to deliver its message and go.

"Zak had better get his ass in gear, this demon is growing impatient, and I'm not sure how much longer I can restrain it. I may have to remove him from the location before the interview if he doesn't hurry up." I told Wendy.

"Crap, why can't they move a little faster!" she commented in frustration.

"I just told the demon if the message was important, he would have to wait for Zak to arrive. Otherwise, the message wouldn't get delivered. He's not happy about waiting, let alone being restrained." I told her.

Its response was scathing, "He's lucky I'm in a good mood; if he doesn't obey me after my message is relayed, there will be a price to pay, I promise!"

"It's almost noon; let's go to the hotel and wait. How are you feeling?" she asked.

"Not too bad, considering I had cancer surgery five days ago. I wasn't about to let the opportunity pass to make this appearance on the Ghost Adventures show; after all, I need the publicity for my books." I said, smiling ruefully.

We got out of the car and went to the hotel lobby. As we arrived, we were met by Cory, the producer who had called me at the hotel.

"I'm not sure how long they'll be at the other side so you might have to wait a while." He said apologetically.

"That's okay. I have a book to finish writing, so we'll be fine waiting here." I told him.

"Listen, Zak wanted me to talk to you about the demon in the basement." He looked a little uncomfortable. "He doesn't want you to remove anything until after they've done their investigation."

"Uh, Okay." I smiled at him while on the inside, I knew that I would never leave town with this particular demon still on the loose.

Cory left smiling, secure that I would do as Zak requested.

What Cory didn't know was the strength and tenacity of this particular old demon. I knew Zak had already encountered him in 2008 at Bobby Mackey's. The Old One told me he had been watching him for the last ten years. A demon doesn't watch you for that long without a very good reason. I was curious as to what its reason was. I wasn't about to ask it; I figured it would tell me when it was darn good and ready.

After an hour, Stuart and his wife Christina arrived. "Have they been here yet?" Christina wanted to know.

"No, we've been waiting for over an hour; did you just get done?" Wendy asked them.

"No, we've been done for 30 minutes. They mentioned filming a 'B roll' down by the pier. But we thought they would do it later. They must have gone there when they left us." She said.

"When Zak and I talked off-camera, I told him about you and what you do, and he seemed very intrigued," Stuart told me.

"Well, it looks like we have to wait for them to get through with that before my interview. Let's get a coffee, and you can tell us about your interview. If I had known, I would have brought my laptop with me. I could have at least worked on my books." I said, sighing.

We spent the next hour discussing the filming and where our next investigation should be done.

Before I came down on this trip, God asked me to give one of my black salt necklaces to Aaron to see his reaction. I told God that the guys don't accept gifts from people, but I knew there had to be a reason for Him wanting me to do it. So, when Aaron came upstairs to talk to Cory, I got up and went over to him.

"Hello, Aaron; God wanted me to give you this necklace for protection," I told him. I could see two negatives next to him and knew he had attach-ments.

"I don't believe in God." He told me.

I said, "That's funny; he believes in you, and so does Lucifer. I told God you wouldn't accept it, but he insisted." I smiled at him, turned around, and sat with my friends.

"Did you see the look on his face?" Wendy asked me. "I could see he was terrified of you. The closer you got to him the more scared he looked."

"That's because he has two negatives attached to him. I'll remove them once we leave here." I told her matter of factly.

"Dam it, that old demon downstairs is trying to rip my head off my neck. My head and neck are so painful it's all I can do to hold my head up." Wendy said, rubbing her neck.

"I wish there were something I could do, but I'm sorry to say it won't get any better until I remove the old demon," I told her, sighing in frustration because the crew was taking so long to get started.

Eventually, Cory let me know they were ready to film. He was a nice young man but shouldn't be anywhere near a negative. Shrugging my shoulders, I reminded myself it was none of my business.

They hooked me up to the microphone and led me outside, where Zak waited. I thought I had only been contacted for an interview, but it turned into a mini-investigation.

Standing outside the Norblad hotel, Zak asked me what a demon seer is.

"What exactly is a demon seer?" he asked.

I looked at him and explained, "The term demon seer comes from my grandmother's Irish ancestors. It is a person who can hear, communicate, see demons in their true form, command them, and, in extreme cases, destroy them. Like the old demon waiting for us in the basement."

The change in the sound and camera crew was almost palpable. They were apprehensive, on edge, and a little fearful.

"Wow, okay, first I want to know some things. Is my crew going to be alright? They won't be harmed in any way, right?" he asked seriously.

I could tell that the safety of his crew was very important to him. "As long as I'm here, they'll be protected, and no harm will come to them."

"How do you know there's a demon in the basement of the Hostel?" he asked curiously.

"I always know days, even weeks, before I encounter one that they are coming. Call it a kind of built-in radar. The demon told me it came here to speak to you specifically and wanted me to relay a message to you." I informed him.

. "What, you're kidding me, right? What does the demon want with me?" he wanted to know.

"I don't have an answer for you. You'll just have to wait until you meet it in the basement. I do know one thing, though. You've met this demon before." I told him.

"Can anyone see the demons in their true form or only you?" he asked seriously.

"I've had more than one person who were mediums wanting to see what I see when I encounter a demon. Only one went through with it and he's never forgotten. It's something that haunts him to this day. It's an experience that he's not willing to repeat." I informed him.

"Why is that? What do you see that's different than what I've seen?" Zak asked curiously.

"If you have to ask me, then you've never seen the true face of a demon. Demons look into your mind, draw on your preconceived image of what you think they should look like, and then amplify it by a hundred-fold when they show themselves to you. I see them in their pure form; I don't know of another person who can see them in this way without having nightmares for a long time. If you look into their eyes, you see pure evil and every atrocity you can ever imagine and more." I said seriously.

"Are you ready to go into the basement?" he asked, ignoring what I had said about his having met the demon before.

"The bigger question is, are you ready?" I murmured under my breath.

We entered the hotel, and to the left was a door that led to the basement. I had been down those steps two months before.

"After you," Zak said, opening the door and motioning for me to precede them.

I hid my smile by keeping my head down. I could feel the atmosphere change as I descended the stairs.

Once we were all in the largest part of the basement, I could feel the crew getting nervous.

"So where is the demon trapped?" Zak asked me, looking around.

"You see that far dark corner on the left side? That's where he is, and he's not happy." I told him, pointing to where it resided.

I walked towards the corner where the demon was secured. Billy Tolley was my cameraman for the duration of the mini investigation.

As I moved toward the demon, I could feel Billy following me. As I moved closer to the demon location, I heard a deep growl but did not react; Billy did.

"What the fuck was that?" He asked me. "I know. I just heard a growl."

"Oh, that was just the demon. Don't pay any attention to him, and he's in a nasty mood." I responded.

"Bring him over here now." The demon snarled at me telepathically.

"Not just yet; you'll have to wait until I'm ready to talk to you," Auriel warned it.

"What about the other door at the bottom of the stairs? Where does that lead?" Zak asked.

"I don't know, let's find out, shall we?" I asked heading back the way we came.

Zak and the crew followed behind me. Opening the other door, I saw a dimly lit passage that seemed to branch out to another area.

"I'll go first; you guys can follow me," I told them, heading down the dimly lit hallway. I could see a few of the creepy crawlies scurrying away from me. *"You had better run!"* I told them creating a vortex to suck them into. I smiled as they were sucked into it, screaming. More creepies were hiding on the far side of the open area.

"Is there anything down in this section?" Zak asked.

"A few creepy crawlies, a lesser demon way in the back, and a small portal," I informed him.

"Where's the portal?" he asked, I could tell he was excited at the prospect.

Moving towards the end of the area, I pointed to the right, where I could see the end of the building, which someone had tried to board up unsuccessfully. There were just enough boards missing to allow someone to squeeze through.

"Aaron, I want you to go down there and see what's on the other side of the boards," Zak instructed him.

"Okay." Aaron walked carefully down to where the board fence was. Sticking his head through to the other side. Pulling his head out, he looked at Zak and said, "Bro, this doesn't feel right; the whole feeling back here is heavy and weird."

"Just get in there," Zak responded impatiently.

Aaron took a deep breath and went inside. "Bro, I don't like it here; I feel surrounded by something." He said nervously and came back through the boarded area.

Some of the others started roaming around the small area.

"I don't like it here; it feels like something is watching me," Billy whispered.

"It's because there's a lesser demon back here with us. But don't worry about him; as long as he's just watching, you're ok." I whispered back, smiling at him. I could tell he wasn't thrilled about having this thing anywhere near him. I can't say I blame him.

"Let's head back to the main part of the basement where the demon is," Zak instructed everyone.

I lead the way back to the larger basement area.

"Are you alright?" Zak asked me noticing my look of preoccupation.

"Yeah, I'm just keeping it at bay," I told him.

"Is it down here now?" he asked.

"Yeah, it's right over there, in the corner," I told him. "A portal was created, a dark portal, and it came through there. It's not very nice; they never are, but this one is especially nasty.

"Can we go near it?" Zak asked.

"Sure," I said, leading him toward the corner where the demon was contained.

"Where exactly is it?" Billy asked.

"It's right in line with this post," I said, using the post I was standing next to as a guide. "You see that box over there? It's between the box and the white streak on the wall." I guided him as he pointed the camera in that direction.

"Can you communicate with it?" Zak asked me.

"Oh yeah, they understand the thoughts. They speak in Aramaic. My brain is hard-wired to understand what they are saying. I had one friend in particular a medium who wanted to see what I see and hear what I hear. I warned him not to look into the demons' eyes. I told him to hold my hand, and he couldn't believe it. He saw what I saw but couldn't understand the language. Only the intent. The intent was to harm me. Then, the language changed to a high-frequency piercing sound. Two huge demons stood a short distance from us. The next thing he knew, one of them started to run towards him. He let go of my hand, breaking the connection, and the image disappeared. I held up my hand to stop the demon. He had nightmares for years."

"Can I try holding your hand?" Zak asked.

"I told you before, not many people can stand to see demons in their true form as I do. It will change you in a way that is not easy to define. I only know that he is not the same as he was before he connected to me." I warned him again.

"Alright, I get it, but I still want to do it." He assured me.

"Alright, but don't say I didn't warn you. You will hear what I hear and see what I see. I'll need to take it away from you once we are through." I instructed him. "The demon is taking this chance to deliver a message to you. I suggest you listen to it. This is an old demon, and they rarely visit the physical realm. If it has a message for you, then it's a warning, and they don't issue them lightly." I warned him.

Holding out my hand, I instructed him to grab hold of it. "Here, take my hand. You won't understand its language as they speak in Aramaic, so I will translate," I informed him.

As our fingers touched, the connection was complete.

"They say you were meant to come here and understand they exist. That they are real and that they can and will hurt you. He wants you to heed his warning because there will be significant repercussions if you don't. They want you to stop provoking them and seeking them out. He has been watching you for the last ten years and judging your actions." Just as I finished delivering the message, Zak ripped his hand from mine.

"Ow, that was weird. I felt a jolt go through me." Zak commented. "At first, there was white light and peace. I tried to keep my thoughts clear then the whole scene went blacker than anything I've ever seen. Through the blackness, I could see it in the corner, just as you said it would be.

"Yeah, the white is the angelic energy that runs through me," I told him.

Zak decided to make contact with the demon using me as an interpreter. "Why did you attack my spine?" he asked it.

I gave him the demon's answer, "It's your weak spot, he says." I relayed the message.

"Does the spinal cord give you power?" Zak asked.

"No, it incapacitates you," I repeated the demon's response.

"Why do you follow people home? Why do you attach yourself to them?"

"Because I can, it says."

"What do you want?" Zak asked another question.

"It says it wants to inflict as much pain and suffering in the physical world as possible. It wants to crush you financially, emotionally, mentally, spiritually, and your health. It has a habit of affecting all those areas."

I could tell the contact with the demon was already affecting the crew, especially Zak.

He decided to ask one last question. "So, will you let us see and hear you? Can you make a sound? Give us a message in whatever language you speak?"

Suddenly, footsteps could be heard on the landing above a small staircase that led nowhere.

"That came from the platform at the top of the stairs," Aaron said and climbed the stairs to confirm there was no one up there.

The demon stopped communicating as I had delivered its message. Whether Zak would heed the warning was questionable. I needed to remove my sight from Zak.

"I just need to remove what I gave you, the ability to see," I told him.

"What? To remove it?" he asked, seeming a little confused.

"Yes, you don't need to see what I see. No one should be able to see and do what I do without having an angelic soul. They would have a lot of mental issues from it." He seemed even more confused, and I knew it was the old demon muddling his senses. "I don't want you to have to go through that. I have lived with seeing these things since I was five." I told him.

"He responded, "I've dealt with them too."

I thought, *"You don't see them like you did today. You're lucky I filtered most of what you saw."* but I didn't say anything.

"I just don't want my stuff being messed with right now." He told me. He appeared to be very out of it at the moment, so I left.

"Okay," I agreed, knowing I would remove it later if he chose not to do it while I was still there. One thing was certain: I would remove the old demon before I left town. After all, there was still a lesser demon and creepy crawlies left to play with. I would remove these, too at a later time.

I left them and went back upstairs to the hotel lobby. There was a sudden activity by the hotel door, and I was just in time to see Zak run from the hotel and into a waiting SUV.

I didn't know it then, but he called Billy about what happened. I found out later when I watched the show what had transpired.

"I feel like I've got no sleep in the last five days. I could go home and sleep for like 12 hours right now. I feel like that lady took everything out of me when I touched her hand. After a couple of seconds, my back started hurting. I don't feel well. I started having flashes, seeing things, and hearing voices that weren't there. I don't think she knows what she's dealing with. I don't think I should have touched her hand." Zak said.

Billy relayed to him the conversation we had off-camera. "Hey Zak, you walked away, but here's what she told me off camera. She said you will hear voices and see things that you shouldn't. She says you can't handle it. With these abilities, demons can reach out and mess with your mind. She said it's imperative that she take away the ability to see and hear how and what she sees. She let you experience it to help you understand how powerful these things are. Maybe you should call her and tell her to shut it down."

I was preparing to leave when the producer Cory came to find me. "Hey, I just got a call from Zak; he wants you to remove the sight from him." He said, looking nervously at me.

"Okay, I'll remove it, where is he?"

"He's returning to the hotel; he'll meet us outside," Cory informed me.

Once he arrived, they put a mic on me, and I went downstairs where Zak was waiting. Taking his hand, I removed the sight from him.

"It's done," I told him.

"Thank you." He said sincerely.

"One word of advice: do not provoke demons; you have no idea what they can do to you or your crew," I warned him. I knew he wouldn't listen to me, but at least I had to try.

Before I left the hotel, I removed the old demon and closed the dark portal. I left the lesser demon and imps there to play with the Ghost Adventures crew. This way, they would have their evidence for the show. Once their filming was done, I removed the rest of the negatives, including the ones attached to Aaron.

CHAPTER TWELVE

AIR FORCE DEMON

In 1981, I was in the Air Force stationed at a SAC base in Spokane, Washington. I was working as a clinical specialist in the emergency department at the base regional hospital. It was around 11:00 AM, and I was four hours into my shift when the telephone rang. One of the other Techs, Win Boggs, answered the phone. There was a short conversation with the person on the other end, and he hung up.

"What's up?" I asked him curiously.

"You're not gonna believe this, but Tech Sargent said one of the men in the barracks he's in charge of hasn't shown up for work for two days."

"So, what are we the lost and found? What does he want us to do about it?" I asked him with a sigh.

"Well, it sounds like they want to go into his room in the barracks to see if he's in there. My guess is they think he might be dead, and they don't want to body. I think that's why they want us to go with them. Sounds like the Tech Sargent is afraid of what he might see." Boggs said, grinning.

"Yeah, I get it; there are those who don't want to see dead bodies. If he is dead, hopefully, he's not still earthbound. You'd better bring a body bag just in case."

"Hey, if he is dead, maybe his ghost is hanging around, and you can have a nice conversation." He joked.

Boggs was one of the very few who knew about my gifts and what I could do. His grandmother is a voodoo practitioner who had gifts as well. When she found out he was working in the emergency room, she worried about him. When he told her about me his grandmother told him not to worry because she had connected with me on the spiritual plane. She told him I was special; her words were 'a defender of heaven'.

Boggs told me he did not understand what she meant by that, but if she told him to keep close to me, that was exactly what he would do.

The hospital where we worked was located outside of the main base, nestled in the base housing area. We got into the ambulance and headed towards the barracks, which housed the LE (law enforcement) personnel. Arriving at the barracks, the Tech Sargent who had phoned earlier was waiting for us.

We unloaded the gurney, grabbed our supplies, and headed for the front door. Once inside, the sergeant led us to a freight elevator located at the end of the building. We traveled silently to the second floor, where he led us to a room halfway down the hall.

"I'll just open the door; I'm not going to go inside I'll wait out here. Just let me know whether he's alive or dead; that's all I want to know." the sergeant stated.

Boggs and I looked at each other and shrugged; we thought the sergeant was a wuss.

The sergeant pulled a large key ring out of his pocket and began sorting through it. It took him a moment or two to find the correct key. Inserting the key in the door lock. He pulled the door open. Standing behind it so he wouldn't have a view into the room. Boggs and I looked at each other and rolled our eyes, getting a firm grip on the gurney, I entered the room first.

Upon entering the room, the first thing I saw was a man curled up in a fetal position propped against the wall. I couldn't tell if he was alive or dead. The second thing I saw was a large demon positioned in the left corner of the ceiling. It seemed to be staring intently at the man on the floor. I ignored the demon, knowing I had to attend to the man. I noticed very shallow, slow breaths coming from him. Pulling out my stethoscope, I placed it on his chest, listening for a heartbeat; I found a slow but steady heartbeat. There was no response from the man to our or the demon's presence.

Turning to Boggs. I told him, "We need to get him back to the hospital right away. He has a heartbeat, but it's very slow, around 40 bpm. If he's been here for at least 2 to 3 days, he's going to be dehydrated."

We lowered the gurney in preparation for the transfer of the young man. Unfolding the man's limp body from the fetal position, we lifted him onto the gurney. As I attended to the man, I could still feel the demon watching in the background. Elevating the gurney, we left the room and headed for the ambulance as we exited the room.

The Sergeant asked, "Is he alive? What happened?"

"We don't have any more information other than he has a pulse and is breathing. You'll have to wait until after he's been examined at the hospital before we know what is happening with him. By the way, does he have a name?" Boggs informed him shortly.

"Airman Chris Tobin, he's a Chaplin assistant." The sergeant informed us.

We headed back down the hallway and entered the freight elevator. I glanced out of the corner of my eye to see if the demon had followed us. I could see no trace of him, but I could still feel him. We loaded him into the back of the ambulance. I stayed in the back with the young man, and Boggs drove the ambulance. Once we left the building. I could not sense the demon anywhere close by. I was hoping that it had moved on. The young man remained unconscious the entire trip to the hospital with no response at all to stimuli.

Arriving at the hospital, we took him to one of the large exam rooms, where we transferred him to the stationary gurney. Once he was settled, I knew the next step would be to start an IV. Boggs and I left the exam room to get the needed supplies.

Once outside of the exam room. I looked at Boggs and said, "There was a demon in the guys room."

"Crap, I knew there was something wrong, but I couldn't put my finger on it. What are you going to do? Is it still around? Did it follow us?" He asked, looking nervously around.

"I couldn't feel it after we left the barracks. I'm hoping it moved on, but I won't hold my breath."

"Well, I do not want to be around if it reappears!" He stated vehemently.

"If it shows up again, I'll have to ask for help from the Legion," I told him.

Gathering the supplies I would need to start the IV, I headed back into the exam room. Just before I entered the room, I felt a big shift in energy, a shift not for the better. Pushing the door open I entered the room to find the demon hovering over the young man. It was blacker than anything you could see in the physical world, its eyes glowing red. The evil emanating from it was enough to make a strong person vomit and run away in sheer terror. I could see it was trying to drain the life force from him.

It looked up as I entered the room, and I heard it telepathically say, "He's mine!"

I could feel a rush of anger fill me it was stronger than anything I had ever been in my life.

Suddenly, I heard a voice that seemed to be coming from me but was not my own say, "This one belongs to us! Leave now while you can, and pray you never run into me again!"

Whatever the demon saw in my face must have convinced it to leave because it disappeared in a split second.

My anger dissipated almost immediately once the demon disappeared. I finished setting up and starting the IV. Just as I finished, the duty doctor entered the room. He examined the patient and ordered some medication to help bring him around. An hour later, at the end of my shift the man was starting to respond to stimuli.

I was off duty for the next two days. I wondered about the change in myself and my voice during the altercation with the demon. I had never experienced anything like that before; it almost felt like someone else was working through me. I was not one to channel, as I did not want to open myself to spirits.

Going back to work on the third day, I decided to stop in and see the young man, Chris, before I started work. I knocked on the door of his room.

"Come in."

"Hello Chris, my name is June; I brought you into the hospital when you were so ill. How are you feeling?"

"Considering what happened to me, I think I'm doing okay. They tell me that someone put some PCP into my soda at a party I went to. It really did a number on me."

"Yes, it's a good thing your body was able to recover; you could have died from the drug."

"You know, I seem to remember this very vivid dream. In the dream, a demon was trying to suck the life out of me, but a fierce-looking female warrior angel came and chased the demon away."

"I think God was trying to tell you that he has your back and that he will protect you from the dark ones. You are a very lucky young man to have the angels watching out for you." I told him.

"I think you're right; he was watching over me."

We talked for a few more minutes then I said goodbye having to report for duty. I found out later that he was discharged from the Air Force because of the trauma of what happened to him.

CHAPTER THIRTEEN

MIRROR PORTAL

It was early June, and I was at home cleaning the house when one of my guardians, my sister Ann came to me.

"June Ann, someone is coming back into your life that you haven't seen in many years."

"Male or female?" I asked telepathically.

"Female, the name starts with a 'J.'"

"Well, I can't think of anyone at the moment. Is she a person that I want to see again?"

"Yes and no, I would say."

"You're being cryptic about this person. I'm not going to worry about it now; I'll deal with it when it comes up." I said, shrugging.

A few weeks passed with no word from my guides about the person with the 'J' name. Then, one day, I got a call from my younger brother Lee, who said he had run into an old friend of mine. It was the woman with the 'J' name. I'll call her Jenna.

"Hey, I ran into Jenna the other day, and she's staying at mom's old house. She's having a problem with what sounds like a haunting."

"What type of haunting are we talking about? That house has never been haunted. If there's something there, she brought it with her." I had a sick feeling in the pit of my stomach. I grew up in that house, and I was never happy there. It held a lot of painful and depressing memories for me. I am sure there's plenty of psychic residual from when I lived there to attract a negative. My mother had a habit of beating you with a baseball bat if you did something wrong. She would grab anything she could get her hands on to beat us. It didn't matter whether it was a board, belt, or her fist as long as it was handy.

"I don't know, are there different types? I thought a haunting is a haunting. All I know is she said something was making noises in the house. Can you call and talk to Jenna about it?" My brother wanted to know. "I stopped by the other day, and I could swear that I saw something black dart across the backyard; it gave me the creeps. She wants to move out of the house as soon as possible."

"I know it's negative; I can sense it. It's more than just your usual run-of-the-mill negative entity. Moving won't help; it's attached to her. It has integrated itself into the walls of the house. I'm not relishing the thought of calling her. Give me the number, and I'll call her once I've spoken with God to see what she needs to do. It may not be today, but it will be soon. How long has she been dealing with this?"

"She told me it's been going on for over eight years. She says they hear scratching and clawing in the walls, growling, and objects are being moved. I know it's negative, but what do you think it is? Could it be a shadow person?"

"No, it's more than that, I'm afraid. Hold a minute; Ann has something to tell me about what's happening." My sister Ann, one of my guides, began talking to me telepathically.

"This demon is crazy; there's something wrong with it, JuneAnn. She invited it in using a Ouija board, and it's been attached to her ever since. Fortunately for her, the demon has integrated itself into the house, making removing it easier. It chose to reside in the house because it was a young, inexperienced demon, making removing it easier."

"Are you still there?" My brother asked.

"Tell her to leave the house for three days and not to return until the morning of the fourth. This way, I can remove the demons without them knowing I am coming. Auriel and the Legion will clear the house."

"You were right; it is more than a negative earthbound entity. I'm sure glad I never went into the house. I had a bad feeling about it. Okay, I'll tell her what to do. But why can't you call her? This whole thing gives me the creeps."

"You have to call Jenna; if I call her, they will know Auriel is aware of them and be prepared. Just tell her I said to leave the house now for three days and not to return until the fourth, nothing more than that."

"But why can't I tell her what you said about the removal?" he asked.

"Because if you tell her it will know, and then it will reattach itself to her, and she'll need to have an exorcism performed. While it's attached to the house, the Archangels can remove it. It won't go willingly, so there will be a big fight. Usually, they cast it back into hell. It's unusual for a demon to travel by itself; they're like coyotes and travel in packs. You say you only saw the one figure?"

"Yeah, that's the only one I saw. Jenna said that sometimes she thinks there might be more than one, but she's unsure."

"There's got to be at least one other one there, but it's hiding for some reason. The one in the house is the stronger, more dominant of the two," I reasoned out loud.

"Well, I'm not about to find out, that's for sure! I'll tell her what to do and call you after she leaves."

"Okay, let her know I'll call her after this is done." And I hung up the phone deep in thought.

My brother called me the next day to let me know she had left the house. I waited a few days for the activity to settle down in the house. This would lull the demons into a false sense of security. They do it to us so that a little payback would benefit them!

Two days later I got the key to the house from my brother. Arriving at the house I could feel three different entities. Upon entering the house, I noticed how eerily quiet it was. Walking through the main level, I could feel the demons watching me and wondering who I was and what I was doing there.

I made my way to the full basement. Once there, I walked into each room, including the closets. I sensed the demons growing restless; their energy seemed to ramp up. I returned to the main level and stood in the living room.

Suddenly, the front door, which was bolt locked, was flung open with a bang rattling the room. A recliner across from me was pushed violently towards me, narrowly missing my legs. When I didn't react, I could feel the entity's anger growing by the moment. A deep guttural growl broke the silence of the house.

Closing my eyes, I merged into Auriel's consciousness to see what demons were in residence. There were three: one old demon and two lesser demons. The old demon was one that Auriel had dealt with in the past; the other two were minor players.

"Is that the best you can do, D******?" I asked him telepathically, sarcasm dripping from my voice.

"Who are you? How do you know my name?" It asked, startled by the fact that I knew his name.

Auriel came forward fully, her countenance one of a fierce warrior pulling her swords out of their sheaths. She stood before the old demon.

"What are you doing here, assassin? I have no quarrel with you!" D****** told her to go on the defensive.

"You called me here by your interference in this woman's life. I will not tolerate your behavior."

"She summoned me; I have the right to be here! You have no right to come to interfere with me!"

"I am tired of dealing with you! Prepare to die!" Auriel said cuttingly.

Auriel swung her sword, making contact with the demon's arm, knocking the sword out of its hand. They fought for several minutes until Auriel brought her sword across the demon's throat.

The two lesser demons screamed, and with one stroke of her swords, they fell silent. Standing quietly and listening, she heard the imps attached to the demons scurrying deeper into the house's structure. I closed my eyes and saw Auriel send a pulse of brilliant white light into the house's structure and the land beneath it. The power of the light killed anything negative in its path.

Once the light finished its work, I scanned for anything negative within the local area. There was nothing left in the building or land.

On the fourth day, Jenna went back to the house. She told my brother it looked like a tornado had gone through the house, but it was lighter, and all the bad feelings were gone. A few days after the removal, Jenna started packing to move.

I called her a couple of days after the removal of the demon. "So, how is it going? Does the house feel better?"

"Yes, it feels much better, but I still want to move. After what I've been through here, I want to escape the memories and start fresh. Is there any way that you can help me? Do you know anyone who has a truck?"

"I have a truck, but I have to work, so it has to be on the weekend. I can ask my older brother Steven if he'll help us. He's staying with me because he has nowhere else to live. We can always use another pair of strong hands."

"Thanks; I'll have everything ready to go when you come on Saturday." She assured me, hanging up.

We arrived the following Saturday to move her things. I could feel that the entity had been removed from the house, but I still felt uneasy near the garage. Once we had finished emptying the house, my brother said, "I left a few things in the garage, and I want to take them back to the house with me."

When he opened the garage door, I felt a negative presence. God may have cleaned the house, but there was still a presence in the garage, which was separate from the house. My brother was already inside the garage, and as I entered it, he picked up a large mirror.

"This is my mirror, and I want to bring it back. I had a lot of things here and now there's only a couple of things left. I want to know what mom did with my stuff." He turned and looked at me with pure hate in his eyes.

Then, I knew for sure that a demon was residing within the mirror. It was influencing and feeding off his anger and hatred for our mother. "You can't take that mirror to my house."

"Why can't I? It's mine!" he said angrily.

"Because it's a portal, and a demon is trapped inside it. I don't want it anywhere near my home. It's already using your anger and hate to strengthen itself." I told him quietly.

He looked at me momentarily and then said, "Well, if there's a demon trapped in it, I'm gonna get rid of it."

Suddenly, we both heard a growl emanating from the mirror. Then, a deep, sinister voice said, "No, you're not."

My brother said, "Oh yeah, let's see how you survive this!"

As I watched in horror, I saw him lift the mirror over his head; his intentions were clear. He was going to smash the mirror, which would release the demon. This was just what the demon wanted. Knowing I could not stop him, I called on the Archangel Michael.

In a split-second Michael appeared just as he threw the mirror into the pickup bed. As it shattered, the demon was released and Michael grabbed it, sending it back where it belonged.

"Listen, don't ever do that again; shattering the mirror was the worst thing you could do. You did exactly what it wanted you to do: set him free." I said to him angrily. "If I hadn't asked for Michael's intervention, you could have attached it to you!"

Although the demon was removed after that day, my brother was never the same. He began to drink heavily, and his anger was ever-present. As the weeks went by, he became more withdrawn and hostile toward everyone, including God. He had always been a weak person who was easily influenced. Encountering the demon had a negative influence on him.

I came home one day and went into the room where he stayed in my house. The room was messy, and I found evidence that he had been trying to burn my new French doors with a lighter. There was also residue of what looked like cocaine.

I could no longer let him stay in my home for fear that he would do something to endanger my family. While he was at work that day, I boxed up his things and placed them in the driveway. When he returned home I confronted him with what I had found.

He thought the demon could not influence him, but he was wrong.

Once the active demon was removed, the physical manifestations ceased, but the darkness in the form of depression and anxiety haunted Jenna. Once the darkness has touched you, you will forever be changed. To this day, she is still haunted by the memory of the demonic attachment.

There are different types of portals. Most portals allow those souls who have recently left the physical body to ascend into the afterlife. There are portals that swing both ways. These portals allow souls to come and go in visitation to the physical world. Then there are the dark portals that someone may have opened using the dark arts or where the veil between the two worlds has worn thin. I have encountered all three types, and needless to say, the dark ones are not my favorite.

CHAPTER FOURTEEN

TO CATCH A DEMON

It was a warm summer night, and I was trying to concentrate on my writing. When I felt intense dread, I could no longer concentrate on the computer screen before me. I closed my eyes and opened myself up to the other side.

"What's wrong?" I asked my guides, Hannah, and Ann, telepathically.

"It's your brother; he needs your help," Ann said.

"Which one? I have three of them, you know."

"The youngest one, Robert."

"Why does he need my help?"

"There is darkness surrounding him. Whatever it is, it is trying to block us from seeing it. We're unsure if it's attached to or someone near him." Hannah chimed in.

"If it's blocking you, it must be something strong, and that's not good. I guess I need to call him and check into what's going on. Obviously, I can't call now, but I'll call tomorrow."

Saturday morning arrived, and I called my sister-in-law to find out if they would be home. The phone rang, and my sister-in-law Susan answered.

"I'm so glad you called; I was going to call you. Something is happening with your brother; he's not acting like himself. He's been moody and argumentative, and I feel like there's something negative around him. Ever since we moved into this house, he's been acting strange."

"Yes, I know, my guides told me there's something negative around him, influencing him. He probably doesn't even realize what's going on. I figured you might be aware of it on some level because of your sensitivity."

"It's not only his mood, but when I look into his eyes, they seem darker and colder. Can you come over and see if you can help him? Do you think it's something that just attached itself to him, or maybe it's in the house? When we moved in, I didn't feel anything right away. It's only been in the last week or two that he has been like this."

"I will come down around noon to see what I can pick up on. It will be your job to make sure he's home. On second thought, don't tell him I'm coming. It might be better for him if he remains clueless about this."

"Don't worry, you know your brother, he is definitely clueless. He wouldn't believe me if I told him about this."

Hanging up the phone, I couldn't shake the feeling that getting rid of this would not be easy. Something told me that this entity would not go willingly.

I went to my brother's little rental house a few hours later. The closer I got, the more I felt the presence of a negative entity. Having never been to my brother's new rental house, I was unprepared for the overall feeling of the neighborhood. I could feel all the negativity that seemed to be emanating from the whole area. Opening my senses, I could pick up on pain, anger, depression, substance abuse, and despair. It almost overwhelmed me at one point, so I shut it out.

"Michael, I think I will need your help with this. I'll need you to watch my back." I reached out to him.

"Not to worry, Gabriel and I are here."

"Thanks for coming."

Stopping in front of the house, I drew more white light energy into myself. The moment I stepped out of the car and onto the ground, I could feel the negativity emanating from the land left behind by violence, pain, and anger. It was an unsettling feeling that could give the negative entity a way into me. I closed down the empathic side of me and quieted my mind.

Walking towards the small house, the air seemed to become thicker and heavier with a sense of internal coldness which filled me. It was the feeling I get when there is a demonic presence nearby. I automatically glanced around and reached out with my psychic senses. I could feel a presence lurking nearby and cautiously knocked on the door.

My sister-in-law opened the door and hurried me inside the house.

"I'm glad you got here now; Robert is returning from the store. See what you pick on when he gets here."

"I already feel it, and he's not even here yet. It's influencing him, but it's not a full-on possession. It's good that I came when I did; it won't like me being here. I have two archangels here with me today, but they stay in the background so that it won't pick up on them. I shouldn't be here when he returns; that will take the demon by surprise."

"Why, what happens if you are here when he gets back? Will there be a fight? I hope Robert doesn't get caught in the middle of it."

"They stay hidden to lull the entity into a false sense of security. If they can catch it unaware, they can grab it, and send it back where it belongs. If it senses the archangels, it will try to escape. If it manages to escape, they will have to track it down, giving it more time to cause problems."

"I think what I'll do is to leave until Robert gets here. You phone me and let it ring a couple of times, and I'll know he's here. Then, I can stand outside and deal with the entity. That way, Robert will never know anything happened at all."

"What a great idea, and since I never told him you were coming, he'll be none the wiser."

"If all goes according to plan, you should immediately notice a big difference in him. I would advise you never to tell him about this; it would be safer for him all the way around if he didn't know what was going on."

"What do you mean it would be safer?"

"Well, if he knew about the entity, he would probably obsess about it; you know what he's like. His worry could possibly attract another one to him, and that's the last thing we want to do."

"That's for sure; he's hard enough to live with as it is without the addition of some demon."

"I'm going to head to the store and get something to drink. Don't forget to call me when he gets home. I'll return and park out of sight when I get your call. I won't have to come in. Being close to him will allow me to deal with the entity."

Leaving the house, I headed for the local store. Arriving at the store, I picked up a water bottle and returned to the car. Opening the bottle, I started to take a drink, when the phone rang. Picking up my cell phone, I recognized Susan's number. I didn't answer and finished the bottle of water I had purchased.

After finishing the water, I took a moment to reinforce my protection, drawing it around me like a cloak. I sent a telepathic message to Michael and Gabriel.

"Michael, Gabriel, I'm ready to return to the house. How do you want to do this?"

"We'll meet you there. When you get there, summon the demon. We'll pop in, subdue it, and cast it down." Gabriel said.

"Let's get this straight; you guys are using me as bait? The last time we did this, we worked together. Why the change? What's different about this? Is there something you're not telling me?"

They exchanged a look and then turned to me. "We didn't want to worry you. This removal is a little different than the others we've done together." Again, they exchanged glances.

"What's different about this one?" I asked suspiciously.

"This demon is much stronger than anything you've encountered so far. We need to ensure that it doesn't escape, so we're using you, as you aptly put it, as 'bait.' What better bait than a light worker?" Michael said, grinning at me.

"The least you could have done was told me about this sooner. There's nothing like waiting until the last moment and springing it on me." I grumbled.

"You've only dealt with the lesser demons until now. This is one of the more powerful old demons, and I've dealt with it before. The last time I dealt with him, he managed to escape me. He will not escape me a second time." Michael said grimly.

"So, you have an old score to settle with this entity. Great, that should make it easier from my point of view. Okay, I'll be your bait; what do you want me to do other than call it out? How close does it have to get to me before you jump on it?"

"All you have to do is get him out in the open, and we'll do the rest. Don't let it get any closer than ten feet. It won't be easy because it's a very old and wily demon. I've been hunting him for some time, and I will ensure I get him this time."

"Okay, let's do this then. You had better be ready to grab him before he gets to me!"

Starting the car, I drove back to where my brother lived and parked at the end of the block. Getting out of the car, I closed my eyes. Opening my mind, I sensed the demon nearby and called out to it.

"Foul demon, I summon you in the name of God almighty and Jesus Christ." I could see the demon in my mind's eye, and it was angry. I wasn't sure if it was angry at being summoned or found out. I saw the entity coming through the wall next to the front door. It had the appearance of a large black mass for a moment. Then, my sight changed, and I saw it in its true form. The closer it got to me, the blacker and denser it appeared, its eyes glowing gold and containing such atrocities that the human brain could never conceive of.

"Foolish, mortal bitch, you dare to summon me? You are nothing, a small, insignificant creature!" it shrieked in rage and disdain.

I didn't have to see the black form to know it was getting closer. The extreme cold and the smell of sulfur were almost overpowering. It was all I could do to keep from throwing up. But I knew that to show weakness was to admit defeat.

"Stupid demon, who do you think you are to challenge me? Are you so stupid that you can't even figure out who I am!" I said, forcing out a laugh. "Are you blind too? Do I have to show you who I am for you to figure it out?"

"I know who you are bitch, nothing more than a puny lightworker." It growled disdainfully, moving closer to me.

"Then you are blind, as well as stupid! Let me show you who I am." Suddenly, my consciousness was pushed aside, and the archangel Auriel came forward. I knew that my soul belonged to Auriel. She was a demon slayer and assassin before she was chosen to be one of the five angels to guard the throne of God. She came forward with a vengeance.

"I always knew some of the demons weren't the most intelligent, but I didn't know you were blind as well." She shouted at the demon. "Michael, you wanted him, and I give him to you now."

"Bitch, you tricked me, you will pay for this!" It screeched at me as Michael and Gabriel each grabbed hold of it, and all three disappeared.

Suddenly, my consciousness returned, and Auriel subsided into the background as quickly as she had come. In the next moment, Michael was back smiling at me.

"You did great, June Ann, and as always, Auriel has perfect timing. I figured she would come out when you were faced with the demon, and I was right." He said, grinning at me.

"Why didn't you tell me this was going to happen? This is the first time she's ever taken over. Although I've always known it was possible, I never expected it to happen so suddenly or completely."

"I didn't want you to know because the entity might pick up on it if you knew what would happen. If it did, we wouldn't have stood a chance of capturing it. We were hoping Auriel would push forward and show herself, and she did." Michael said, grinning at me.

Laughing, Gabriel said, "She never could resist a good demonic fight. I sure miss the old days when we were all together as avenging angels." he sighed, "Those were the days."

"Alright, you two, enough. Next time, you need to figure out how to tell me what's happening before I put my neck on the chopping block."

"There won't be a next time because I will teach you how to bring Auriel out when you need her help. It may take a while, but we'll get you there." Michael said, smiling. "How about that, Gabriel, the three of us back together again, just like old times."

They both laughed as if sharing a hilarious, secret joke. Shaking my head in amazement, I left them laughing and headed for the front door of my brother's house. I could tell from how they said it that I would be lucky to survive their 'help' Auriel or no Auriel."

CHAPTER FIFTEEN

SCREAMS IN THE DARK

It was late on a Friday night, and I was just about to go to bed when my guides, Ann and Hannah, appeared before me with a message from God.

"June, we have an important message from God," Ann informed me.

"You need to get a piece of paper to write this information down," Hannah said.

"Okay, just give me a minute to get a paper and pencil." Rummaging through some of the drawers in the room, I finally found a paper and pen. Sitting down, I prepared to take notes.

"We told you in 2011 that 2012 was the beginning of the great awakening. People would become more spiritually aware, and the light would spread worldwide. As the light spreads, the darkness tries to push it back." Ann said.

"Yes, I remember. You said it would get worse before it got better. I assumed it would be a gradual spreading of the light, and the darkness would be pushed back gradually. Something has changed. I hate to sound like a Star Wars groupie, but I've felt a change in the force."

Hannah and Ann exchanged a knowing look. "That's why we've appeared to you in the physical world. God sent word to all guides and guardians of light workers. We need to inform you that from September of this year through March or April 2013, darkness will increase worldwide. During this time of great darkness, you will see an increase in violence, crime, drug use, death, paranormal activity, and psychological and emotional instability."

"Wow, no wonder I could feel the change. So, is there anything special I need to do to combat the increase in the darkness?"

"Yes, God has given us instructions for a new, stronger form of protection. He wants you to create a special batch of black salt. It is not your usual black salt; this preparation is ten times more powerful. You will need powdered sandalwood, dried sage leaves, sweet grass, charcoal, and sea salt (Dead Sea Salt preferred). First, lay out dried sage leaves, sweet grass and charcoal on a cookie sheet. Using a mist-type spray bottle, spray the mixture with holy water. Set the cookie sheet in the sun and allow the mixture to dry. Once the mixture is dry, place the sage and sweet grass mixture in a fireproof container to burn the mixture until there is only ash left. After the mixture cools, transfer it into something you can grind into powder. You can use a mortise and pestle to pulverize the ashes. Blend the charcoal into the ashes until you have a fine powder. Blend the charcoal mixture into the salt."

"As you create the mixture, repeat these words: 'I bless the salt in the name of God, Jesus Christ, and the Holy Spirit. Let all those who use this salt mixture be protected from anything negative.' It would be best to make enough black salt to give to anyone within your circle of light. They must lay a line down around their home and carry a small amount on them or in their vehicle. This will protect them during this time of darkness and beyond."

"Okay, I'll make up the black salt as soon as possible and send it to everyone within my circle of light. Tell God thank you for the heads up and the protection."

"He says you are welcome. One more thing June, be careful when you're away from home. The dark side is very strong during this time, and you may see and hear things you have never experienced. Remember this: do not acknowledge any creatures of darkness during this time."

Just after I was given the recipe for the black salt, the time of darkness began in September 2012. During the time of darkness, I had a one-on-one encounter with some unusual creatures of the dark. It was 7 PM on a Friday night, and I had just gotten off work. Darkness had fallen, and the weather was cold and wet. Usually, even at 7 PM, there was quite a bit of traffic on the way home. That night, while driving home, I didn't encounter one other vehicle on the road. The air itself felt heavy, and the darkness seemed even darker. I was only a couple of miles from work when the light in front of me turned red.

Sitting at the light, I had an overwhelming feeling of being surrounded. I could feel intense negativity, but I couldn't get a good picture of it.

Opening myself up, I saw dark creatures with heavy, leathery wings and large talons thrashing through the air. As if that wasn't scary enough, a sudden horrendous screaming filled my head. It was like nothing I had ever heard before. The screams were a mixture of evil, darkness, and pain. It left me feeling cold to the very core of my being.

I remembered my guide's instructions not to acknowledge the creatures of darkness, so I closed myself off from the other side. I'm unsure how long I sat at the traffic light, but I didn't seem to be aware of the time passing. Even though I had closed myself off, I could still feel the creatures following me as I drove towards my home. I really didn't want them to follow me home. Even though I had my protection in place, I still worried about my family and animals, so I opened my mind again and called out to Michael the Archangel for help.

"I am here; have no fear; these are the minions of the dark one, and I will deal with them."

Just before I arrived home, I felt the darkness lifting and knew they were gone. I hope never to hear the screams of demonic minions again.